C000264355

Forty 2 Days

Georgia Le Carre

Forty 2 Days

(Book 2 of the Billionaire Banker series)

Published by Georgia LeCarre

Copyright © 2014 by Georgia LeCarre

The right of Georgia LeCarre to be identified as the Author of the Work has been asserted by her in accordance with the copyright, designs and patent act 1988.

All rights reserved. No part of this publication may be reproduced, stored in a retrieval system, or transmitted, in any form or by any means without the prior written permission of the publisher, nor be otherwise circulated in any form of binding or cover other than that which it is published and without a similar condition being imposed on the subsequent purchaser.

All characters in this publication are fictitious, any resemblance to real persons, living or dead, is purely coincidental.

ISBN: 978-0-9928249-0-7

You can discover more information about Georgia LeCarre and future releases here.
https://www.facebook.com/georgia.lecarre
https://twitter.com/georgiaLeCarre
http://www.goodreads.com/GeorgiaLeCarre
http://www.georgialecarre.com

"I hurt myself today
To see if I still feel.
I focus on the pain
The only thing that's real."

—Hurt, Johnny Cash's version
http://www.youtube.com/watch?v=SmVAWKfJ4Go

Table of Contents

One

I edge up to the counter, my hands clammy, my stomach in a tight knot. The woman manning it smiles efficiently. She is wearing the bank's uniform; a striped shirt, a navy blazer and matching skirt. Her black name-tag has Susan Bradley printed in white.

'Thank you for waiting.' Her voice is iceberg lettuce crisp. 'What can I help you with today?'

I run my hands down the skirt of my gray suit. 'I have an appointment to see an officer about a loan. The name is Lana Bloom.'

She consults her computer screen. 'Ah! Miss Bloom.' Her eyes move upwards. Meet mine. No smile there. Just avid curiosity. 'Take a seat, and I'll let someone know you are here.'

'Thank you.' I walk towards the nest of gray-blue chairs she indicates. I perch on the edge of one and watch her.

'She's here,' she announces into the phone, and returns it to its cradle. Then she does an odd thing—without turning her face in my direction, sneaks a look at me from the corners of her eyes, catches me watching, and looks away quickly, almost guiltily.

I feel the knot in my stomach grow tighter. Something is wrong. Perhaps the manager has looked at my business plan and decided against the loan. It shouldn't be too surprising. I have no experience and no collateral and, as my mother used to say, banks will only lend you an umbrella when it is not raining outside.

I clutch my bag in sweat-slicked hands, take a deep breath and very firmly urge myself to be calm. There is always Plan B—Billie and I will simply start small and build the business brick by brick. Our progress will be very slow, but we will survive, and perhaps if we work extra hard, one day we will thrive. With or without their money we will get by. My chin goes up a notch.

An Asian lady in a dark suit comes out of a closed door. She looks at me, eases into another smile that doesn't quite reach her eyes, and asks, 'Miss Bloom?'

I stand nervously and smooth down my skirt. Here goes nothing. I touch my hair self-consciously. Hope the wind outside has not wrecked it too much. In an attempt to look older and more professional Billie scraped my hair back into a severe bun and colored my lips a dark plum. She said it has the effect of making me look like a sophisticated flamenco dancer, but I think it has simply made me look pale and gaunt.

'This way please.' The woman waves her hand in the direction of the stairs and starts walking towards them. I frown deeply. All the other people waiting with me have been shown into one of the cubicles downstairs. Upstairs, I have not seen anyone go. Why am I going upstairs? The woman's clunky heels make a hollow sound on the uncarpeted stairs. The sound reverberates in my chest. The feeling of dread in the pit of my stomach increases.

We go through a door that requires a code, and I realize that we have entered the area that only staff members are allowed into. Another employee passes us and glances at me curiously. We walk down a corridor of offices. Near the end of it the woman turns around and faces me. There is an oddly speculative expression on her face.

'Ready?' she asks. It seems a strange thing to ask.

Bemused, I nod.

She knocks once, pulls open the door, and holds it ajar for me.

I enter, a sunny smile plastered all over my face, and freeze. My jaw drops, my stomach lurches in my body. I am in a nightmare. *Ah, but haven't you waited for this for a long time?* Always my heart knew it was not over. One day I would see him again. I didn't know how or when or why—just that I would.

And I have rehearsed this scenario in my mind countless times but in different circumstances. Where I am dressed seductively and have run into him in a

nightclub or while I am accidentally, purposely loitering outside One Hyde Park where he once told me he lives. But never, never here at my local bank. Not in a million years. I am so shocked my mind actually goes blank. I blink.

Oh! But to be caught this unprepared!

'Wait,' I want to scream to the Asian lady, 'there has been some mistake,' but my mouth is frozen open, and even my slow-moving brain knows there is no mistake. I have not been shown to this room by accident. I am here because this man wants me here.

The door closes quietly behind me.

Two

'Hello, Lana,' Blake says from behind a desk. His voice is still the same. Jack Daniel's on ice. Smooth. A bite hidden somewhere in its amber depths.

A shiver runs down my spine.

He looks at me with a tight jaw and unreadable eyes. He is even more beautiful and raw than I remember. An impossibly splendid, impersonal god. But there is something different about him too. Some harshness that wasn't there before has crept into those hooded, intensely beautiful eyes. Some faint lines about his mouth.

The shock to my system of seeing him so unexpectedly is so great I am unable to say or do anything. Robbed of all coherent thought I simply stand there slack-jawed: a fool, greedily drinking in the sight of him. For I, have spent many a long, lonely night, the heat of the desert all around me, trawling the net looking for any mention of this man.

For months nothing.

Then one day on a conspiracy site—a brief article that he got engaged to Victoria Montgomery, daughter of the fourth Earl of Hardwick. I sat back, my body in an unbelievable turmoil. Insane jealousy is like red-hot lava. It poured into my gut, carrying with it the terrible, terrible sensation that I had lost something irreplaceable.

There was a small picture of them taken at a restaurant. So grainy there was nothing to be gleaned from it, but I had stared at it for a long time that day, and gone back to it again and again. As if it held some clue to a mystery I didn't understand. Slowly, I began to notice things, the coffee cup, his hand on the table close to, but not touching hers. Victoria's face upturned to him, hard to tell her expression, but there was the impression of great devotion and determination. I had rubbed my seventh-month belly slowly. The circles my hand made comforted me. That life is not yours. That man is not yours. Has never been. But this baby is all yours. The molten lava cooled, formed its black crust. The fan droned on. In the next room, my mother slept, blissfully unaware of my deep sorrow.

'Have a seat,' he invites smoothly.

But I dare not move. My legs are pure jelly. I close and then open my mouth, but no words come. I swallow and try again. The song 'Baby Did A Bad, Bad Thing' starts playing in my head. Shit. I am in trouble. Bad things always happen when that song starts playing in my head.

'What are you doing here?' My voice is barely a whisper.

'Processing your loan application.'

'What?' I know my expression must be without intelligence, like those worn by beasts of burden, at the very least slow, but I cannot stop the slackness.

'I'm here to process your loan application,' he repeats patiently.

Sounds logical, but his words are rocks in my brain. Process my loan application? I shake my head to dislodge the rocks. 'You don't work here. You don't process tiny little loans.'

'I'm here to process yours.'

'Why?' And then a stupid thought occurs to me. Later I will think back and slap my forehead at my own naivety, but at that moment it fires me into action. 'So you can turn me down? Don't bother. I'll show myself out,' I say hotly, and begin to turn.

He stands. 'Lana, wait.'

I look all the way up at him. Strange! He even seems bigger, taller.

'I am the one in the entire banking industry most likely to extend you this loan.'

I continue to stare dully at him. How I have longed to set eyes again on this man. And how I have missed the sight of him. How truly beautiful he is.

'Please take a seat.'

Dazed I look at the two chairs facing him, but I do not move. My thoughts trawl through treacle. Nothing makes sense.

'How did you know I would be here today?'

'A nifty little software that flags your name if it matches your date of birth whenever it comes up in the banking system, and, of course, the fact that you began using your account again less than a week ago.'

I can't think straight.

'Is all money in the Swiss account gone?'

I nod. 'But why are you here?' I ask, even though I already know the answer to that.

'Same reason as before.'

'For sex.'

'Sex?' he hisses. 'God, you have no idea, have you?'

He is angry. Angrier than I have ever seen him. I stare at the transformation in disbelief. What shocks me the most is the expression on his face, drawn, hard, his jaw clenched so tight the muscles in his neck stand out. His eyebrows are two straight lines. The urbane man who fed me caviar and quietly upgraded my mother to first class is gone, vanished, replaced by this stranger with furious, mistrustful eyes. His breathing seems to grow harsher as he advances towards me. He stops a foot in front of me.

At that moment he emits tremendous power. Electricity crackles between us. He holds my gaze steadily for heart stopping moments and I see the battle in his eyes. The emotions that wage for control. I flinch as he draws even closer. Until we are inches apart and the scent of him invades my senses. Nobody else I know smells like him. The smell of old money, Rupert called it. For one unguarded instant carnal lust glitters in his eyes. Then he lowers his lids and masks it. But I have already seen it, the potency of his desire for me. It heightens my perceptions. Drenches me with wanting and lust.

I feel my skin tingle in response. My lips go numb and my throat becomes so dry words would scratch it. What could I have said anyway? *Oh, Blake, I'm so sorry?* I reach out a trembling hand to him.

His reaction is instant. 'Don't,' he rasps, stiffening.

Shocked, I retract my hand. I have damaged him. The knowledge spreads like a dull ache in my chest. 'Please,' I whisper, stupidly, helplessly.

He bends his head towards my face. My eyes are riveted on those sinfully sexy lips. I remember their taste, their passion.

'Dishonest little Lana,' he murmurs, his breath hot against my skin. He runs his hands down the smoothness of my neck into the collar of my blouse.

I begin to tremble. He watches his own fingers slip a button out of its hole and then another. He spreads apart the joined material so my throat, chest and the lacy tops of my bra are exposed. His cold furious eyes return to mine. The breaths that escape my lips are suddenly shallow and quick. He smiles possessively. He knows the effect he has on me.

'You were by far more when you squeezed into that

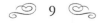

little orange dress and your fuck-me shoes and went looking for money. Look at you now; you're flapping around inside a man's jacket. Two hundred thousand and you don't even buy yourself a nice suit.'

He tuts. 'And this…' He raises his hand to my hair. 'This ugly bun. What were you thinking of?' he asks softly, as he plucks the pins out of my hair and drops them on the blue carpet. Bit by bit my hair falls around my shoulders. Without moving his feet he reaches back to a box of tissues on the table. Takes one and starts wiping away my lipstick. Meticulously. From the outside in. He throws the stained tissue on the ground.

'That's better,' he pronounces.

I stare wordlessly up at him. He looks as if he wants to devour me. All the time we have been apart is wiped away. It is like we have never been away from each other. This is the man I belong to heart and soul. Without him I have been an empty shell going through the motions.

'Lick your lips,' he orders.

'What?' I am horrified by the cold command, and yet electrified by the sexual heat his order arouses in me. My nerves scream.

His jaw hardens; his eyes are steely. 'You heard me.'

The tension in his body communicates itself to me. It simmers between us. Desire ripples through me. My thighs clench tight with excitement and my heart flutters like a crazy thing. This is how he is in my recurring fantasies. Demanding, possessive, taking, raging with sexual need. But the sane logical part of me doesn't want to comply. The argument between my brain and body is pure torture. In the end, yeah right, as if there was ever any doubt, my body wins. So what if I slip and fall on that slick road. It is only for a moment.

I lick my lips slowly.

He eyes the journey my tongue undertakes avidly. 'That's more like it. That's the mercenary bitch I know.'

One moment he is standing there cold and insulting, and the next he has thrust a rough hand into my hair and pulled my head back. I gasp with shock, my eyes wide, his dark. Like a desert storm he descends on my parted mouth. There is no time even to pull one's cloak about oneself. So sudden. So unexpected. He tastes wild, the way the first drops of rain in the desert taste. Full of minerals. Bringing life to all it touches.

He kisses me, as he has never done. Roughly, painfully, violently, purposely bruising my lips, his mouth so savage that I utter a strangled, soundless cry. The change, the extent of his anger, is impossible to comprehend. He is different. There is no longing. Only an intense desire to hurt and have his revenge. This is not the same man. My actions have unleashed something uncontrollable. Something that wants to hurt me. Alarm bells go off in my head. It occurs to my fevered brain that he is ravenous, starving. Then for some strange reason an image of him eating thin, almost transparent slices of cheese on biscuits flashes into my mind. How civilized he was. Then. Before I betrayed him.

I taste the fury in his kiss: blood.

And my mind screams—this is abuse. A moan gets caught in my throat, struggles vainly, and then escapes. My hands reach up to push him away, but my palms meet the stone wall of his chest, and as if with minds of their own, push aside the lapels of his jacket and grip his shirt. I know what once lived beneath the shirt and I want it. I have always wanted this man. As if my hands splayed across his chest have communicated my total submission, the kiss changes. His tongue gentles, but demands more surrender.

The fingers grasping my hair hurt my scalp. I feel the pain vaguely, but more than that I feel myself begin to drown in that vortex of sexual desire. The violent, throbbing need between my legs finds its way into my veins and flesh. Every cell in me wants him inside me. I am on fire. One year of waiting has made me hungry for him. I want him. I want him thrusting that enormous dick of his deep inside me. For a year I have dreamed of him inside me, filling me. I know how good he can make me feel. My body tries to burrow closer to him, but I cannot get closer; his grip on my hair is relentless. Desperately I push my hips towards him towards what I know will be delicious hardness.

As if that is some silent signal he puts me casually away from me. And I am thrust back in a shitty back office in Kilburn High Street. What the fuck am I doing? He casually props himself against the desk, folds his arms across his chest and looks at me calmly.

I cannot return the insult. I am a mess. I stand there frustrated beyond belief, breathing hard, the blood pounding like an African drum in my head. My knickers are wet and between my legs I ache and pulse for him. With every weak and trembling part of me I want him to finish what he started. I want him so bad it is shocking. I clench my hands at my sides and try to get myself under control. I look at him, how cool and collected he is, as he watches me struggle to regain some measure of composure.

Then he smiles. Oh! Cocky. He shouldn't have done that. I feel maddened by the taunting smile. How dare he? He just wanted to humiliate me.

And then I see it. Not so fast, Mr. Blake Law Barrington.

I take two steps forward, reach my hand out and put a finger on that madly beating pulse in his throat. It drums into my skin. The frantic beat is carried away by my blood up into my arm, my heart and into my brain. Years later I will remember this moment when we are connected by his beating pulse. We never break eye contact. His eyes darken. Now he knows that I know— my need may be obvious and easy to exploit, but he is not as unaffected as he pretends to be. He was testing his own limits of control, but it hasn't been as easy as he expected.

'Is it sex when I want to see you come apart?' he asks bitterly.

A breath dies in my chest. I take my finger away from

his throat. 'What do you want, Blake?'

'I want you to finish your contract.'

I drop my face into my hands. 'I can't,' I whisper.

'Why not? Because you took the money and ran, while I lay in a hospital bed.'

I take a deep breath and do not look up. I cannot look up. I cannot face the condemnation in his eyes. I did not keep my word. But I had a reason, one that he can never know about.'

'I was cut up to start with,' he says.

I look up, shocked, mesmerized. Contrary to his words his face is detached, calm, cold, so cold.

I shiver. 'You were cut up?'

'Funny thing that, but yes I was.' He shakes his head as if in disgust. Whether it is with me, himself, or both of us, I cannot tell.

'I thought it was just a sex thing for you,' I murmur. My world is all wobbly. He was cut up! Why?

'If you wanted money why didn't you ask me?' His voice is harsh.

'I...' I shake my head in defeat. I cannot redeem myself.

'You made a serious miscalculation, didn't you, Lana, my love. The honey pot is here.' He pats the middle of his chest. I look at the large male hand. Something inside me twists. Once that beautiful hand with its perfectly manicured nails roamed my body, swept my legs apart and entered me. Dear God!

'But not to worry. All is not lost.'

My gaze lifts up to his mouth. It is thin and cruel and moving.

'You did me a favor. You opened my eyes. I see you now for what you were...are. I was blinded by you. I made the classic mistake. I fell in love with an illusion of purity and loyalty.'

I raise my face up to his. Blinded? In love? With me?

'If I had not bought you that night you would have gone with anyone, wouldn't you? You are not admirable. You are despicable.'

'So why do you want me to finish the contract?' I breathe.

'I am like the drug addict who knows his drug is poison. He despises it, but he cannot help himself. So that we are totally clear—I *detest* myself. I am ashamed of my need for you. '

'The...The...people who paid me—'

'They can do nothing to you. My family—'

I interrupt. 'What about Victoria?'

A sudden flash of anger gleams in his eyes. 'The fact that I need the feel and taste of your skin is my shame and private hell. Don't ever bring her into our sordid arrangement. Her name on your lips makes me feel sick. She is the one pure thing I have in my life. She stood by me through...everything.' He pauses, his lips twisting. 'I actually told her about you and gave her the option of leaving me, but she refused. She is wiser than me. Far wiser than I gave her credit for. She said you are just a sickness and one day I will wake up and the sickness will be gone. Until then…you owe me 42 days, Lana.'

My God, he really hates me. I close my eyes unable to look into the censure or revulsion glittering in his. He cannot know how much his angry words have cut and wounded me. I had guessed he would think badly of me, but I never imagined he would so utterly loathe me. I never realized that I had hurt him so deeply. I honestly thought it was a sex thing for him. That I was just another in a line of many. In my defense he had never given me to understand otherwise.

Now he hates me with a passion. And there is not a single thing I can do about it. Victoria has shown herself to be a formidable foe. I can never tell him what really happened. I am on very shaky ground. I will have to be very careful. I have too much to lose. I hang my head. I need to think.

'Name your price.'

My head snaps up. 'No,' I hear myself say. This time my voice is very strong and sure. 'You don't have to pay me again. I will finish the contract.'

'Good,' he says, but he frowns, and for one second I see not just confusion that I refused his money, but something else—relief? No, that would be too weak an emotion for the wild thing leaping into his eyes. Then it slips away seamlessly. A seal that leaps and disappears into the blue ocean.

'Back to business then,' he murmurs, and, turning away from me, goes around the desk, and takes his position behind it. Back to the way I found him.

Three

I watch his toned, powerful frame slide smoothly into the black swivel chair and open the file in front of him.

'So, you're setting up a business?' The sudden professionalism in his voice is like a bucket of cold water in my face. I take a shocked backward step. We were somewhere totally different a moment ago. Awareness of his potent masculinity in that small utilitarian room is still prickling across my skin. So, he wants to play. Cat and mouse. First the cheese and then the claw and teeth.

I go forward. Position myself in front of one of the chairs facing the desk. When I feel the edge of a chair against the backs of my knees I sink into it. 'Yes, Bill... Billie and I are.'

'Ah, the inimitable Bill,' he says, looking up, the hot gaze completely replaced by a remorseless mask. 'Why didn't she come with you?'

'She thought her tattoos might put the loan officer off.'

He smiles lopsidedly. 'You girls have it all covered, don't you?' he says, but I can tell straight away, he has a soft spot for Billie. It twists my heart. I wish my name would soften his face like that.

'That reminds me. How is your mother?'

The breath gets sucked out of me. 'She passed away.'

He stills, his eyes narrowing. 'I thought the treatment was working.'

I swallow the stone lodged in my throat. 'The treatment worked.' The words catch in my throat. 'A car. Hit and run.'

His eyes flash. For an instant I am looking back into the past. We are all sitting around my mother's dinner table. There are fresh flowers on the table and our plates are full of Persian food. Chicken with fruit and rice. My mouth is full of the smoky flavor of dried chilies. Blake is being charming and my mother is laughing. Her laughter fills the room and my heart. Hardly I heard her laugh in my life. I did not realize how happy I was then.

'I'm sorry. I'm so sorry to hear that, Lana.'

His pity is my undoing. The scene before me blurs. I blink furiously. I am not going to crumble in front of him. I can feel the waves of grief beginning in my body. I have not yet cried. Oh shit. Not now…please. I stand suddenly. So does he. I put out a hand, a warning—do not come any closer—and I run to the door. I need to get outside. My only thought is to escape. Not let him see me break down, but he is already at my side. He grabs my arm. I twist away from him, but his grip is too firm. He doesn't know it, but he is part of the great pattern of my terrible grief.

'This way. There is a staff restroom,' he says quietly, and opening the door leads me down the corridor. He does not look at me, and I am grateful for that. Hot, uncontrollable tears are streaming down my cheeks. I did not cry when my mother died. For three whole months I could not cry. There was so much to do, but now the silent tears are flowing unchecked, and the huge sobs are on the way. I can feel them shaking my innards, threatening to burst out.

He holds open the toilet door and I rush in. The door closes behind me. Inside are white tiled walls and cubicles made of plywood. An ugly place. Perfect for what I have to do. I grip the ceramic basin, stuff my fist into my mouth and, doubling up, wait for the screaming sobs. They don't disappoint in their ferocity. They are long and hard and ugly. Full of regret and recrimination and blame. For so long I believed that my mother would die of cancer. Year after year of watching her suffer and still not being able to let her go in peace, and then when she is bright and full of life again, and, when I am least expecting it, she is gone. Just like that. Without warning. I never even had a chance to say goodbye. In the end she was cruelly snatched away from me. I don't know how long I was in there, but I buried my mother there.

Alone, in a toilet reeking of industrial bleach.

Finally, I lean against the sink exhausted. I look in the mirror. What a right mess. I look horrible. I blow my nose, wash my puffy face. My eyes and lips are red and swollen. I straighten. I button my blouse to my neck. I know it is cowardly, but I decide at that moment to scuttle away. Just walk down the corridor and leave. The bank has my address and he will find me, but by then I will be different. I will have repaired the walls of my fortress. I will be strong. He cannot hurt me. But then I remember Billie waiting at home.

'Well, did you get it?' she will ask.

I close my eyes. I'm not going to let her down. I'm going to say, 'Yes, I got it.'

I pull open the door and he is standing in the corridor outside, staring at the floor, his hands rammed deep into his trouser pockets.

It is the oddest thing. It reminds me of the first time we met. When I had bawled my eyes out in a toilet and come out to find him waiting for me. He looks up, still frowning. The door shuts behind me as he strides towards me. The last time I had six inch heels that lifted me to almost his eye level. Now I am left staring at his brown throat.

'Are you okay?'

I nod.

'Tom will take you home.'

I lift my eyes up to his. They are strange, liquid with some emotion I cannot comprehend. 'No,' I say. My voice comes out oddly terse. I had not meant for it to be like that. 'Let's get this loan business out of the way.'

A shutter comes over his face. I realize then I have just confirmed his thoughts about me. I am the gold digger who will do anything for money. Anybody else would have exploited this opportunity for softness. I am filled with regret, but it is too late. He is the tide that is going out and cannot be recalled. His eyes return to cold and distant.

He nods and we go back to the clinical office. I sit opposite him and he takes the swivel chair. It is a parody. He knows it and so do I.

He looks down again at my loan application form. 'Baby Sorab?'

Oh. My. God. What the hell am I doing? I am playing with fire. I feel my heart thump so loudly in my chest he must surely hear it. The fog in my brain clears. It is no longer just me. Cat and mouse? I can play this game. He has nothing to lose. I have everything to lose. So I will be the winner. He will not beat me. I school my features, shrug carelessly. And then the lies begin to drop from my mouth so smoothly even I am surprised. Until today I never realized what an accomplished liar I am.

'Yes. We thought it was a good name for our business.'

'Why baby clothes?'

'Billie has always been good with colors. She can put red and pink together and make it look divine, and since, Billie had her baby this year we decided to make baby clothes?'

'Billie had a baby?' he asks, obviously surprised.

I look him in the eye. 'Yeah, a beautiful boy,' I lie straight-faced.

His lips twist derisively. 'You girls sure have it figured out. I suppose she is now being housed courtesy of the British taxpayer?'

I say a silent apology to Billie. 'I believe we have had this conversation before.'

'OK,' he says.

'OK, what?'

'OK you got the loan.'

'Just like that?'

'There is one condition.'

I hold my breath.

'You do not get the money for the next 42 days.'

'Why?'

'Because,' he says softly, 'for the next 42 days you will exist only for my pleasure. I plan to gorge on your body until I am sick to my stomach.'

I swallow hard. 'Are you going to house me in some apartment again?'

'Not some apartment, but the same one as before.'

I lick my lips and surprise myself. I never knew I could think so fast. That lies would come so easily to me. 'There is one small complication. Billie goes to see her girlfriend three, no actually, four nights a week and I take care of her son.'

He doesn't miss a beat. 'Tell Laura what you need for

the baby—cot, pram, bottle warmers whatever. The baby can stay at the apartment.'

I stare at him. 'Are you serious?'

'Do you have a better plan?'

I pause. My mind racing. 'One more thing. Billie must be able to come to the apartment.'

'Done.'

'And Jack. He is the baby's godfather.'

He looks bored. 'Anything else?'

'No.'

'Fine. Have you anything planned for tomorrow?'

I shake my head.

'Good. Keep tomorrow free. Laura will call you to go through the necessary arrangements with you.'

'OK, if there is nothing else...'

'I'll walk you out.'

Heads turn to watch us. Their eyes slide off when they meet mine. I feel my face flushing. Hell, I'll never be able to come back here again. I see the bank manager hurrying towards us, the material of his trouser legs slapping against his ankles. Blake raises a finger and he stops abruptly. Blake pulls open the heavy door and we go into the late summer air. It is a gray day, though. Drizzling slightly.

We face each other.

'Why did Billie call her baby Sorab?'

'It's from the great epic Rustam and Sorab.'

'Yes, I am aware where it is from, but why did she

choose it?'

'It was a tribute to my mother. It was my mother's favorite story.'

'Hmmm… That is the most admirable quality in you. Your unshakeable loyalty towards your mother.'

For a moment we look at each other. I realize that I have never seen him in the light of day. Not even in this dull light. Strange. We have always met during the day at the apartment and only ever gone out at dusk or at night. And in the light of the day his eyes are storm-blue with moody gray and black flecks. A gust of wind lifts his hair away from his head and deposits it on his forehead. Unthinkingly, I reach a hand out to touch the unruly skein, but he jerks his head back as if dodging a wasp.

'This time you won't fool me,' he bites out.

We stare at each other. Me, astonished by how close to the surface his fury lives, and he, contemptuously. My hand drops. I feel exhausted. There is a ton of bricks inside my chest. Cotton wool inside my head. I can't think straight. I look down the road at the bus stand. 'I'll see you tomorrow then,' I say.

'Here's Tom,' he says, as a Bentley pulls up along the curb.

I shake my head. 'Thanks, but I'll take the bus.'

'Tom will drop you off,' he insists, and I have a flashback of him from the first night we met at the restaurant. That same inbred sense of confidence and superiority.

'No,' I snap. 'Our contract doesn't start until

tomorrow. So today I'll decide my mode of transport,' and I swing away from him.

His hand shoots out and grasps my wrist. 'I will pick you up and put you in the car if necessary. You decide.'

I feel anger bubbling inside me. 'And I'll call the police.'

He actually laughs. 'After everything I have told you about the system—that's your answer?'

I sag. 'Of course, who will believe me if I claim that a Barrington tried to force me to take a lift.'

'Please, Blake.'

'Very well. Tom will go with you on the bus.'

I don't argue. I simply turn around, open the car door, get in, slam it shut and stare straight ahead.

'Good morning, Miss Bloom. It's good to see you again,' Tom greets, pretending not to notice my puffy face.

'It's good to see you too, Tom.'

'How have you been?' he asks as the car pulls away.

'Fine,' I reply, and twist my neck back to look at Blake. He is standing on the sidewalk where I left him. His hands are hanging by his sides and he is staring at the moving car. On the street teeming with some of the most dispossessed people in Britain he stands out. Tall, impressive, separate from the crowd, a ruler; and yet he looks alone and abandoned. I remember what he told me a long time ago.

I trust no one. No one.

Four

The traffic is bad and the car crawls slowly down Kilburn High Street. I stare blankly out of the window. I know I'm not dreaming this. This is actually happening and yet...it has a dreamlike quality. The street looks the same only there are many people staring at the car and into it, at me. Their eyes seem unfriendly. The rich are resented here. I feel restless and disturbed. I need a bit of time to think. Walking always helps. I ask Tom to drop me off by the shops.

'Are you sure, Miss? I don't mind waiting, while you pop in. I'm free until much later.'

'Thanks, but I'll be fine, Tom. I'll probably see you tomorrow, anyway.'

Tom nods. 'All right then. Mind how you go.'

I enter the newsagent and buy a bottle of vodka and a packet of cigarettes for Billie. Then I walk home slowly, taking the long way home so I pass by my old house. I stand on the street in the drizzle and look up at it. At the blue door where we once lived, my mother and I, for so many years. Some of them happy, but most of them filled with stress and worry and fear. Now she was gone.

For a moment I stand there, my face upturned, pretending that my mother is still there. That I could, if I wanted to, simply go up those stairs, put my key in the door, open it, and find her in the kitchen. Bald and thin to the point of skeletal, but happy to see me. Then the blue door opens and a child about seven years old comes out. She has brown hair cut very short.

From the interior a woman's voice yells, 'And I want change from the fiver.'

The girl doesn't answer. Simply slams shut the door and runs to the top of the stairs. She is so cocky she reminds me of Billie. I hear her shoes clattering down the stairs. She runs past me, dirty stained top, yellow shorts and brown legs. And suddenly, I am racked by a sense of deep nostalgia for those times when Billie and I ran free. Summer days. Fingers sticky with ice lollies. Not a single responsibility in sight. I watch the girl turn down the road towards the shops. Then I slowly begin to walk towards the tower block flats where Billie and I now live.

It is a horrible place, far, far worse than this small, friendly block. If Blake saw where we live now, he would literally have a heart attack. All his worst nightmares are realized here. Prostitutes work the underpass and there are fights and stabbings when the pubs clear at night.

Their drunken shouting and cursing floats up to our flat. Inside our block it is no better. The lifts perpetually smell of stale urine and the stairwells are littered with blood-filled hypodermic syringes and used condoms. Kids play among the needles in the morning.

I live here, but in my heart I am absolutely determined that it will only be temporary. I intend to work hard, make our business work and, hopefully, by the time Sorab is old enough to walk the three of us will be out of here. A sign says no ball games and no dumping of rubbish. In defiance the place is littered with empty cans and someone has simply tipped a badly stained mattress over one of the long balcony walkways of the tower.

I pass the children playing on the concourse.

'Hey, Lana, we saw you get out of a big car by the shops. Whose car is it?'

'Never you mind,' I tell them tartly.

'Somebody's got a sugar daddy,' they sing, and I am surprised anew by how clued up these kids are. At their age, my innocence was complete, my childhood totally unsoiled by any adult knowledge.

One of them breaks from the group and sidles up to me. 'Go on, give us a pound to buy some sweets,' she cajoles. She has a head full of bouncing brown curls.

I look down at her. 'Does your mother know you are begging for money?'

'Yeah,' she pipes up immediately, standing her ground without the least trace of embarrassment.

I look into her eyes and feel sad. I know her mother.

A hard-faced woman with six kids. Each one from a different father, all dirty and unkempt. For a split second I consider teaching her not to beg, to have pride, and then I give up. I know in my heart it is pointless. I wish a different future for her, but she is already infected by the generation before her. In her round, beautiful face walks the shadow of a drop-out, perhaps even an alcoholic. A blight on society through no fault of her own. I reach into my purse and give her a pound. She grasps it in her small, hot palm and runs off in the direction of the shops, calling after her. 'Thanks, Lana.'

I skirt the weeds and step onto the cracked concrete. Moodily I kick a Coke can out of my path and round the block. I look up to the second floor of the ugly gray block and see Billie standing on the long walkway balcony outside our door. She is smoking a cigarette and leaning against the metal railing. One of her bare feet is curled around a metal bar. Her hair is no longer white, but flaming red. She changed the color and the style last week when she broke up with Leticia. It is now cut very close to her head on one side and falls longer on the other. She must have just got out of the bath, for her hair is still wet and slicked to her head. She does not see me.

I run up the smelly stairs and step on to our level. She looks up from her contemplative stare and watches me. I step over discarded toys, a tricycle, a plastic bucket and spade, and then I am standing in front of her.

I grin. She kills her cigarette on the metal railing. I

fish out the vodka. She grins back. Hers is real, mine is not.

She takes the bottle from my hand. 'Really?'

'Really,' I say.

She puts the bottle on the ground, grabs me around the hips, and sweeps me off my feet, laughing. Her joy is so infectious I have to laugh.

'Put me down before you drop me over the balcony!'

Instead of setting me back down she whirls me around a couple of times, carries me over our threshold and kicks the door shut like a man, before setting me down on the dining table.

'You. Are. A. Fucking. Genius,' she says. Then her face undergoes a sudden change. 'Oh, shit,' she cusses and dashes outside. And she is just in time too. 'Oi you,' I hear her shout. 'Touch that bottle and you're dead.' There is the sound of little feet scuttling away and Billie comes back into view cradling the vodka bottle.

I slip off the table. 'How did it go with Sorab?'

'The usual, you know, eat, shit, sleep, repeat,' she says, and thumps the bottle on the table.

'Let me have a quick peek,' I say, and go into my bedroom. I stand in front of his crib, my heart heavy with sadness. He has no one, but me. He will never know his father. I have denied him his father and a life of unimaginable riches. I push the guilt away. Not now. Not yet. For a moment I think of Blake standing alone in the crowd. We are all of us alone trapped in our own version of hell. I gently trace my finger on his sleeping arm and go outside.

Billie is sitting at the table.   The vodka bottle is unopened.

I slip my jacket off. It is too big for me and swings from my shoulder.   I open the fridge. 'I'm going to make some pasta. Want some?'

'No, had a couple of Turkish Delights.'

'Bill, you can't survive on leftover pizza, jam, and chocolates, you know.'

'It's not me who looks like a walking skeleton.' She stares at me daring me to contradict her.

I close the fridge door and face her.

'You know, when I saw you walking home with the plastic bag from the newsagent I didn't dare believe, because I could see that you had been crying. I'd like to think you cried because you were so happy but that's not it, is it? Want to tell me what really happened?'

I sit opposite her. 'Blake was there.'

Billie pulls forward with a frown. 'There where?'

'At the bank. He processed our loan application.'

'Don't. You're going to make me cry.'

'Can you bite back the sarcastic remarks for one moment?'

She raises her hands, palms facing me.

'Apparently he has been monitoring my account with the intention of making contact.'

Billie opens her eyes wide. 'Wow! That's tenacious.'

'He wants me to finish the contract.'

Billie closes her eyes in a gesture of extreme

exasperation. 'Oh God! You agreed or we wouldn't have got the loan, would we?'

'Yes,' I say, but before I can tell her more she leans forward, her chin jutting out aggressively.

'Lana. Are you completely crazy? Have you forgotten what that bloodless troll he is engaged to and those reptilian entities masquerading as his family did to you the last time? They closed ranks and kicked you out of the fucking country. Anyway, didn't she make you sign in blood never to go near her man again?'

I flush. 'No, simply that I must never make contact with him again. I didn't.'

'Yeah, she'll appreciate the difference.'

'As a matter of fact, Blake said that he has told her about me and she is prepared to wait until he is over his infatuation with me.'

'And you believe that?'

'Well, it *was* something like what she told me.'

'If you believe that then you definitely should stay away from him. You are not equipped to deal with such lethal cunning.'

'I won't come into contact with her. It's only 42 days.'

'We don't need the money, you know? We can always start small. We talked about this. In fact, it was unlikely that you were ever going to get the money without collateral or business experience. It was only an off chance. We'll do without it. In fact, that might be more fun.'

'I didn't do it for the money,' I say very quietly.

There is a moment of shocked silence. Billie looks at me as if I have lost my mind. And in a way she is right. I am risking everything.

'Fuck me, Lana. Have you forgotten how difficult it was for you to get over him?'

'I'm not over him.'

'Exactly. So why walk into the lion's den *again*? Look at you. You are already just a shadow of yourself. Why put yourself through it? Besides the spectacular sex, that is.'

I try to smile and don't succeed. I feel my chin and lower lip begin to tremble. I press my lips together. 'You don't understand. I *owe* him. He was good to Mum and me, but I didn't keep my word. I should never have taken Victoria's money. It was wrong. I knew that the moment I saw it sitting all fat and jolly in that Swiss bank account. I'm not a Swiss bank account person. It was only when I gave it all away to that hospice that I felt better. I will only feel right again when I finish what I started. Until then I will never be able to close this door.'

'And Sorab? Are you going to tell him about *him*?'

'Of course not. They would take my son away and turn him into a cold-eyed predator, like Blake's father and brother.'

'So what happens to Sorab then?'

I squirm a little. 'I told Blake Sorab was yours.'

'Right,' she says slowly, obviously unable to get her head around such an idea.

'He thinks you did it to jump the welfare queue and get a flat.'

Billie grins suddenly. 'So you didn't tell him that as a child I wanted to have my entire reproductive system removed and replaced with an extra set of lungs so I could smoke more.'

I shook my head.

'What does all this translate to then?'

'You keep Sorab here for three days of the week and I keep him at the apartment for the other four days.'

Billie draws a deep breath. 'What does he imagine I am doing for the other four days?'

'Spending the night at your girlfriend's place.'

'Jesus, I'm a shit mother, aren't I?'

'Do you mind terribly?'

'I don't give a monkey's what he thinks of me, but are you OK with being apart from Sorab three days a week?'

My little heart is breaking at the thought but I put on a brave face. 'Well, it *is* only for 42 days and I was thinking that three weeks of that time I could say you are on holiday and Sorab is too young to go with you.'

'And you think he'll believe that?'

'Quite frankly, I don't think he cares enough to ponder the matter too deeply.'

'I don't want to take the philosophical upper hand here, but if it'll all be over in 42 days, isn't this all a bit... unnecessary?'

I trace my fingernail along the wood grain of our kitchen table. We bought it in a charity shop for twenty pounds. It has two cigarette burn marks on the surface, but I rather like it. It has character, a story to tell.

'I know you think I am being foolish, but have you never had someone touch you and you go up in flames? Or that odd sensation as if your bones are melting and your ears ring like bells in your head?'

'No,' she says flatly. 'And judging from what it has reduced you to... No thanks. I enjoy my self-control. My ability to say no and walk away from a situation that screams danger or abuse ahead.'

'Don't you miss Leticia, Billie?'

'Yes, I do, but... 'She looks at me meaningfully... 'Unlike you I have never had to crawl around the floor with missing her.'

I lower my eyes. Once many months ago when I first left the country I was reduced to crawling on the floor, but that intense pain passed. His reappearance, though, has awakened new realms of need and craving.

'I can say no, but I still miss him, Bill. I miss him like crazy. Even if there is no hope, I still want whatever I can have. I want him on any terms. I actually find it impossible to resist him.'

She sighs elaborately. 'OK, it is your life. When does this charade start then?'

'Tomorrow.'

'I guess we won't need a babysitter for Friday night, will we?'

I make an apologetic face. 'Sorry. Can you babysit tomorrow?'

'While you bang Banker Boy? Sure, why not. I hope that kid remembers what I have done for him when he grows up.'

I smile gratefully.

She fills two glasses with vodka and pushes one towards me. 'Here's to Sorab.' I don't want a drink. I am all churned up, but we clink and down. The alcohol burns the back of my throat. This is no celebration. Not for me and not for Billie. When our eyes meet again, hers are unsmiling; they warn me I am making a dreadful mistake.

Five

By nine o'clock the next morning, Sorab is fed and bathed and I am nervously checking my mobile to see if the battery is low, but it is fully charged and the reception is good. Blake's secretary's brisk, efficient voice comes through at 9:05.

'Good morning, Miss Bloom.'

'Hi, Mrs. Arnold.'

'Is this a good time to talk?'

'Yes.'

'Good,' she says briskly, and then falters for a second. 'I…uh… How have you been?'

'Fine, thank you.'

'That's good. Are you still on contraceptives?'

'No.'

'Oh!' It is clear she cannot understand why I have come off them.

Again the lies trip off my tongue so easily they

surprise me. 'I have been in Iran. There was no need for them. Besides they are difficult to buy over there.'

'I will schedule an appointment with the nurse for a repeat prescription.'

'OK.'

'Next you will meet with the lawyer and then Fleur will take you shopping, and afterwards you have an appointment with the hairdresser, followed by appointments at the nail and wax bar.'

Suddenly I am swamped with a sense of déjà vu. I've done this before. Definitely. First time I was naïve. Stupid. That first kiss, it had blown me away, but now I know... I am the 'unnecessary, unwanted thirst'. The man who thirsts for me also despises me.

But then I thought it was all a fantastic adventure. A romantic dream. How I had jumped in with both feet. All I knew about him and his family was what Bill had read out to me from the Internet. Now I have done my research, sitting alone and pregnant by a window in Iran and I know a lot, a lot more about the great Barrington clan.

I know for example that there are no fewer than a hundred and fifty-three species or subspecies of insect which bear the name Barrington, fifty-eight birds, eighteen mammals and fourteen plants including a rare slipper orchid, three fish, two spiders and two reptiles. Numerous streets around the world and dishes have been named after them too. The only dish I still remember is the one with prawns, cognac, and Gruyère on toast.

They are the twenty-first-century Medicis, offering patronage to artists, writers, and architects. I learned about the houses they have donated to the people and the staggering amounts of money they have expanded into beneficiaries ranging from universities, hospitals, pubic libraries, charities, non profit institutions and archaeological digs. But Blake had already explained how the very rich play the philanthropic game to me. Steal from millions over a long period and give a small portion back as a taxable gift.

Over the weeks I came to realize that Blake's words were true. *If you see it in Wikipedia or a mainstream news outlet then we have planted it.* That everything I read and saw about the Barrington family and history was part of a picture, a false picture. They wanted the world to believe the bogus biographies that they themselves had commissioned, all of which declared their family as a once great dynasty that had since lost most of its wealth and influence. It was the picture of a benign, powerless house that jealously guarded its privacy.

Then I came across a Youtube video of Blake's father. There he was not the cold-eyed man who wanted to arbitrarily dismiss me to the toilet so he could talk to his son. Dressed in an expensive cashmere coat and metal rimmed glasses he worried about the world economy in a mild mannered way. His opinion: more austerity measures should be implemented worldwide before any recovery could be achieved. His silver hair made him look like someone's grandfather, but as I watched him I felt a cold shiver go up my spine.

At his transformation.

At the benevolent role he had so easily and effectively slipped into. If I had not seen the frosty arrogance with which, the blue stones had snubbed me I would never have believed these two men were the same person, but it gives chilling credence to Blake's warning that nothing in his world is as it seems to those in mine. That was when I began to search through the conspiracy sites. And they were rife with 'information'.

The Barringtons were blamed for everything from secretly starting the American Civil War in order to capture the monetary system, precipitating the American bank panic of 1907, to duping Congress into approving The Fed in 1913, to funding the Bolsheviks and Hitler. They were even accused of having a hand in the assassination of Kennedy. I gave up after a while.

There was one thing they got right, though.

They refused to believe the fairy tale that the Barringtons were a declining dynasty, whose members could not even make the Forbes rich list. As far as they were concerned the Barringtons were one of thirteen old families. Through complicated structures of off-shores companies they owned all the debt of all the countries. They were trillionaires and the true rulers behind governments and world organizations. To be a Barrington is to be a modern Croesus, a twentieth-century Midas.

'Is it all right if Tom knocks on your door at 10:00

am?' Laura Arnold asks.

The state of the lift flashes into my mind and I feel ashamed. 'No. Just ask him to call me on my mobile when he gets close to the flat. I'll come down.'

'All right then. Have a nice day, Miss Bloom.'

I thank her and end the call. As I place the phone on the dining table Billie walks in. Her eyes are half-shut. She goes to the fridge, takes a mouthful of orange juice straight from the carton and turns to face me. Her face is unsmiling.

'What time are you leaving?'

'Less than an hour.'

'Right,' she says.

'What would you do if you were me, Bill?'

'I don't know because I don't have all the facts, do I?'

'What do you mean?'

'You took the money and disappeared on him, no note, no goodbye, while he was unconscious in hospital after he had risked, if what you tell me is true, his precious life to save your lowly one. So in his eyes you must be the worst kind of gold digging slut that ever walked English soil. Instead of wanting to jump your bones shouldn't he just put it down to a lucky escape and thoroughly detest you by now?'

I put my head down. I feel ashamed that I have not told Bill the whole truth. 'You're right, he does detest me, but I'm like an itch that must be scratched.'

'Hmmm… There's something wrong with this explanation too—scratched itches get worse.'

'OK. He called it a disease.'

'For fuck's sake, Lana. What are getting yourself into?'

I close my eyes. I am making it worse. 'Look, Bill, it is not as bad as it looks.'

'Make it look better then.'

'I can't. All I can say is, I have to do this. I know I left him, but I have never ever stopped wanting him. There is not a single day that has gone by when I have not thought of him and longed for him. I don't fool myself that I can have him. I know I can't, but these 42 days are mine and nobody and nothing is taking them away from me. So he wants to punish me. Let him. A slap from him is better than nothing.'

Bill's mouth is hanging open with shock. She looks at me as if she has never known me. 'Are you going into some kind of sick sado-masochistic relationship?'

This time it is easy to meet her eyes. 'Blake doesn't know how to hurt me. Even if I asked him to, he couldn't. He believes he can, but he can't. I know that. You've met him. What do you think?'

Bill sighs. 'I liked him,' she admits finally.

I smile, but inside I am incredibly sad. I feel as if I can never touch real or lasting happiness. Everything gets taken away. 'Yes, I got the impression he likes you too.'

Bill turns red.

'Are you blushing, Bill?'

'If he ever tries anything funny, you're out of that sick

contract in a flash,' she says gruffly.

I nod. She has just ensured that I will never tell her the whole story.

.

Six

The appointment with the nurse is quick and painless.

Next stop: the solicitor's offices. I get shown into Mr. Jay Benby's room by his secretary. He stands in greeting. I look around. Everything is exactly the same.

'How are you, Miss Bloom?' he says, half-rising from his chair, the same trust-me-I know-what's-best-for-you smile slowly slithering into his face like he is showing off his pet snake.

I drop my eyes to his turquoise ring and ask, 'Where do I sign?'

He draws himself to his full height. 'I must remind you, Miss Bloom, about the importance and the serious implications of what you are about to sign,' he begins with sanctimonious arrogance, but I cut him off. Last time I was the young thing that came into his office all big-eyed and intimidated by his legal jargon. Not this time.

'Mr. Benby, we are both being paid to be here. We can pretend you are better than me, but why waste our time?'

His eyes narrow dangerously.

Ah, I have offended him. Good.

His movements are sharp and jerky as he opens the contract on his desk to the required page, puts a black and gold fountain pen on top of that page, and pushes the whole shebang towards my end of the desk. Truth is we both know that I don't have to be here. The contract I have already signed is for life. Of course, he can't figure out why I am here, I see that in his speculative eyes, but I know exactly why I am here.

This is part of my humiliation.

I take the pen. It is cool and smooth in my fingers. I unscrew the cap, sign and date the document, then push it back towards him.

'Are we done here?'

He nods stiffly, his anger very firmly held in check. I am Blake Law Barrington's woman, at least for the next 42 days. Untouchable. I turn around and leave.

A small Boots paper bag is sitting in the back seat of the Bentley. I thank Tom , stuff the contraceptives into my rucksack and turn my head to look out of the window. London has a different air from Kilburn. Less desperation, more bustle. The people are different too. They haven't given up. They still believe in their pursuit.

It makes their eyes hard. The way all city people's eyes are. I press my hand to my stomach. I am nervous. I don't know what tonight will be like. So far it seems as if Blake has recreated the day of our first night together. Our first night together still burns in my memory. I replay it in my mind and it causes my thighs to clench together with a mixture of excitement and anticipation.

This time, I think, I will hold my own.

Fleur is waiting in the reception area for me. She walks towards me, smiling, polished and elegant, exactly as I remember her. She embraces me warmly. Then she holds me away from her and says, 'It is wonderful to see you again, but you have become so thin. Have you been all right?'

Suddenly I want to cry. I couldn't cry at all for weeks, but since yesterday the smallest acts of kindness make me want to bawl my eyes out. I bite my lip and blink back the tears.

For a moment Fleur registers an expression of surprise, but she is not a PR executive for nothing. She smiles brightly and making a crook out of her left arm invites me to slip mine through hers. We walk together out of the glass doors. 'Shall we start with some cosmetics?'

'I don't need new cosmetics, Fleur. I've hardly used the stuff you got me the last time. Not much call for it in Iran.'

She turns her face towards me. 'It is bad enough that

women have to put chemicals on their faces, at least let it not be old and toxic. Six months is the maximum that you should keep your cosmetics once opened,' she says firmly, as we exit into the weak sunlight.

We get my cosmetics on the ground floor of Harvey Nichols. Besides the nudes and soft pinks Fleur picks out a scarlet lipstick. 'I am informed that you will be going to the opera. This will be perfect for the black dress I have in mind.' She passes a credit card over to the sales assistant and turns to me. 'Have you been to the opera before?'

I shake my head.

Fleur smiles. 'Well, then it will be a new and wonderful experience for you.'

We get into the lift.

'There is a dress here which you absolutely must try on. It is a dream.'

We are passing a glass showcase when Fleur stops so suddenly I slam into her. Grabbing my hand she yanks me down into a crouched position with her. I stare at her without comprehension as we hunker down behind the showcase. She puts her finger to her lips, smiles weakly and to her credit manages an insouciant shrug.

My first thought is that she has spotted someone she wants to avoid, but the next moment I hear a snooty accent ask, 'Don't you have it in cerise?' An icy claw of horror clutches my stomach. I must have paled or looked scared because Fleur's fingers tighten on my hand and her eyes shoot out a silent, but clear warning to make no sound.

I swallow hard.

The voice is saying something else I do not catch, but it is moving away. Fleur tugs at my hand and starts crawling away. If I was not so shaken it would have been funny. Both of us on our hands and knees in Harvey Nichols! Once when Billie had come barefoot here in the height of summer security had her forcibly ejected. But Fleur is not just anyone. Fleur represents big business, repeat business.

A matronly woman looks at us with widened, disapproving eyes, but then she recognizes Fleur who gives her a small wave. She nods almost imperceptibly and stares ahead. As soon as we reach the end of the long showcase Fleur stands and, pulling me with her, walks quickly out of the department. We go down the stairs and exit the store. Outside Fleur doesn't wait for Tom, but hails a black cab. We get into it and she tells the driver to take us to Kings Road.

Then she sends a text message to Tom to meet us there and turns to me.

'I'm really sorry about that, but it is better that we did not meet her. I take it you know her?'

My hands are trembling. I nod. I am in a state of extreme shock. Of all the millions of people in London I could have to run into, why her? And on the first day of my contract. I understand it to be a bad omen, a warning that I am making a horrible mistake.

Fleur's beautifully manicured hand grasps mine.

'Don't worry about it. It was just bad luck. We will shop in Kings Road instead. There are wonderful places there too. In fact, sometimes I think I prefer it.'

I shake my head. 'I don't want to shop anymore, Fleur. I just want to go home.'

Fleur's eyes change. I see pure determination shining between her extravagant lashes. This is a woman who will not allow anything to stand in her way. I start to admire her anew. She is resilient in a way that I am not.

'You can't go home, Lana. You are committed to this day. We have appointments that we must keep. Victoria is not as powerful as you or she believes. She cannot take away from you that which is really yours.'

'What do you mean?' I ask shakily. I am actually filled with fear. I have lost so much. All I have left is Sorab and if I am careless in any way at all he will disappear like a mirage in the desert.

'My position does not allow me to say, but do not underestimate Blake Law Barrington. He could surprise you yet. Besides, don't you think that women who blame the other woman are stupid? The other woman owes them no allegiance. Look to your own man. He is the one who has betrayed you. Get angry with him, if you dare.'

I nod. Fleur is right. I have done nothing wrong. I kept to my agreement. I left the country for a year. I did not approach Blake. He came looking for me.

'Good,' Fleur says with an encouraging smile. 'Here is what we will do. We will go to my friend's boutique and find something for you to wear tonight and tomorrow I will have some clothes that I think will be perfect for you sent to your apartment? And you can choose what you want and return the rest, OK?'

'OK.'

'I will reschedule your hairdresser's appointment and Laura will push all the other appointments up accordingly.'

In a daze I hear her call the celebrity hairdresser and effortlessly get him to come into the salon four hours earlier than scheduled. People bent backwards to accommodate a Barrington's needs. After that she calls Laura.

'Slight change of plans,' she says. 'Mmnn. Tell you about it later. We are going to the hairdresser's at 1:00 pm. Push all the other appointments up accordingly.' A pause while she listens and then she says, 'Right. That's fine with me. Speak later.' She turns to me. 'All right?'

'All right.'

'Lunch first?'

I am not hungry, but I nod unhappily.

She takes a deep breath. 'If you promise you will never tell anyone what I am about to reveal to you then I will tell you a secret.'

I promise quickly.

'It is very important that you do not tell anyone, especially Blake, or you could drop both Laura and me into some extremely foul smelling stuff.'

'I won't tell anyone. Especially Blake.'

'You are more important to Blake than you think. Sometime after he met you last year, when he was about to go into an important meeting, he called over his shoulder and told Laura to hold all his calls. But then he turned around and said, "except for Lana".'

'Laura was very surprised by the request. You see, never before had he given her such an instruction. Not even for his father or brother. "Is that for just this meeting or for all day," she asked. "Until I tell you otherwise." But here is the most surprising thing of all: Blake Barrington has never told her otherwise.'

The first thought in my mind. That was before.

'Don't make the mistake of thinking that is because he has forgotten. Blake never forgets anything. Not even the smallest details.'

I nod. Perhaps he did care. Perhaps he will learn to care again.

'I did not want us to meet Victoria not because I am afraid of her, but because I think it is unnecessary. It is unnecessary for you and unnecessary for her. She has overestimated her importance; you have underestimated yours. Be confident. Things are not always what they seem.'

A business call comes through for Fleur. She asks if I mind her taking it. I say no and spend my time looking at the shoppers on the street, my stomach rolling with anxiety.

The car comes to a stop outside a brightly painted corner shop called Bijou.

Fleur pushes open an old-fashioned door and a quaint bell tinkles. A waft of carpet deodorant rushes out to greet us. The small shop is so crammed with clothes, jewelry, hats, bags and shoes and so different from the usual pared down designer shop that Fleur usually takes me to that I actually have the impression of having stumbled into Aladdin's secret cave.

A well-preserved small woman of indeterminate age stands from behind an ornate desk and comes forward to greet and air kiss Fleur on both her cheeks. Her laughter is a sophisticated, heavy smoker's rasp. She has that sort of European chic that comes from teaming box jackets in bold colors with numerous ropes of pearls.

I am presented to Rêgine.

She smiles at me, gives me the once-over, and bustles Fleur and me towards a couple of red velvet chairs. When we are seated, she turns the sign on the door to closed and begins running around her overcrowded shop humming to herself. She comes back with three different outfits.

'Try that one first,' suggests Fleur pointing to a fabulous knee-length white dress with a high mandarin collar, three jeweled cut-outs in the shape of leaves in the chest and slits up the thighs. I take it from Madame. The material is the softest wool.

'Only girls with very slim arms can wear the cheongsam,' says Fleur.

'Qui,' agrees Madame Rêgine.

I go behind a heavy velvet curtain, where there are

three full-length mirrors. We have no long mirrors at home. Billie goes to Marks and Spencer's changing rooms to see herself nude. I strip down to my undies. I can see that I am too skinny. My ribs and hip bones are showing. Not a good look. I used to look better before. Immediately I begin to worry if I will please Blake. I remember how attracted to my body he was. How he used to tell me to take my clothes off, and watch me. Simply watch me with hungry, fascinated eyes as if I was the most beautiful thing he had ever seen. What if my body no longer excites him?

'Hey, we want to see,' calls Fleur with a laugh.

'Coming,' I say, and slip into the dress. I zip up and stare at my reflection. Wow! I cannot believe how well the dress flatters me. It makes me look like I have curves. I turn my head to look at my side—the slit that comes to mid-thigh is at once subtle and sexy. Feeling reassured, I pull back the curtain.

'Magnifique!' sighs the throaty voice.

Fleur grins like a Cheshire cat. 'You look beautiful, Lana,' she says and I know that she is being sincere.

'But wait… I have the perfect shoes,' calls Madame, and rushes off to the back of the shop.

She returns with a pair of shoes that are encrusted with similar stones as the ones that edge the leaf-shaped holes in my chest. They are like Cinderella's glass slippers. Only the right girl can fit into them. I take them from her and step into them. The shoes fit perfectly—she must have an excellent eye.

The powdered face smiles cunningly. 'Aaa…but wait…. You must have your hair up.'

She plucks from a large vase three jeweled pins and expertly holding my hair up inserts the pins into it. The European madam, whose age I am slowly having to revise upwards, claps her hands and declares with finality that it is, 'Absolument fabuleux.'

I look into the mirror and I have to agree. Absolutely fabulous. The dress is truly amazing. I have never felt so glamorous or sexy in my entire life. I look at Fleur and she is smiling.

'No one can take what is truly yours away from you,' she says, and I smile.

We come out of Bijou and Tom is waiting for us. He puts all our packages into the boot and takes us to the celebrity hairdresser.

'You let your fringe grow out,' Bruce the celebrity hairdresser accuses.

'I was living in Iran. Women are not allowed to show their hair in public. It was easier to let it grow and pull it all back into a bun and throw a scarf over my head,' I explain.

'Ah, that takes excellent care of my next "have you been anywhere nice?' question.'

I laugh. I like him. He's a rare one, a tough guy hairdresser with a good British sense of humor. And he has a strong determined jaw and eyes that are subtle, but surely undressing me. If I am not totally in love with Blake I could fancy him.

'But honestly,' he continues, 'what the devil possessed you to go live in that godforsaken country?'

'My mother hails from there.'

'Ah! I hear it has very beautiful tiled baths.'

'It has.'

He puts a hand out and touches my cheekbones. 'You have lost weight. A fringe alone will be too harsh. I will feather your hair from your mouth onwards to return that lost softness.'

And he does.

Fleur gives the jeweled pins to the girl who takes over the job of drying my hair and instructs the girl to put my hair up. 'But no hairspray,' she says and winks at me. 'Men don't like hard hair.'

The girl is finished and I am a marvelously different.

It is also time for Fleur to say goodbye. I feel almost tearful. She is the only one who seems to be on my side, rooting for me. She kisses me on the cheeks. 'All will be well. Just be yourself and nothing can be more beautiful.'

Back at the waxing salon I learn that Rosa has moved back to Spain. A stout German woman with reddened hands and nails bitten to the quick takes me into the treatment room. There is no talk about jam sandwiches consumed in front of the TV or a clever son who is in art school, only a silent, ruthless dedication to bald skin. Gertrude strips every single hair from my body. When I am all over a sharp shade of red and the last offensive hair is gone she heaves a large of sigh of satisfaction.

Unlike Rosa she does not offer to do my eyebrows for free. That was from another time. When life was generous to me.

My nails are too short for a French manicure. The girl asks me if I would like acrylic nails and for a moment I am tempted—I have never had them and they seem rather fun—but then I think of accidentally scratching Sorab's tender skin while I am changing his nappy and I refuse. She waves towards a shelf full of nail varnish.

'Choose your color.'

'White,' I say. 'I will have the white nail polish.'

In the car I admire my nails, how pretty and clean they look. 'Tom,' I say. 'If you give me the key to the apartment you can drop me off at my place, and I'll take a cab later to the apartment.'

'Oh no, Miss Bloom that would be more than my job's worth. I got an ear bashing for dropping you off at the shops the last time. I can take you to your place and wait downstairs until you are ready to go to the apartment.'

He drops me off at the entrance and parks by the dark staircase to wait for my return.

Seven

Billie is sitting at our dining table when I enter. The baby's basket is sitting on the table beside her. Surrounded by pens, watercolors, and crayons, she is bent over a large sketchpad in deep concentration. Hair is falling over her forehead and I feel a great surge of love for her. She looks up and smiles.

'Wow! That's a seriously cool hairstyle,' she exclaims, and springing up comes to hold my hand and twirl me around.

'So you like it?' I probe, self-consciously touching my fringe.

'Yeah,' she says emphatically. 'If he won't have you, I will.'

I laugh and go towards the basket. 'Is he asleep?'

'Nope.'

Sorab is waving his little arms. I reach into the basket and lift him into my arms. He is wearing something

Billie designed and made from scratch, a bright red and yellow romper suit with big blue cloth buttons that look like flowers.

'Hello, darling,' I say, my face creasing into the first joy-filled smile since I left the house.

He stares at me with his intense blue eyes for a few seconds before he breaks into one of his deliciously toothless grins.

Over my shoulder Billie says, 'Shame he will have to grow up to be a man.'

I turn around and look at her meaningfully.

'What?' she asks.

'Your dad's a man.'

'That remains to be seen,' she says, and moving towards her drawings, says, 'Come and see this.' I follow her around the table. I put Sorab into the crook of my arm to get a better view of her work. She has drawn a girl's dress. It is not in the usual pale pink normally reserved for baby girls, but banana yellow with green apples all over it. I have never seen anything like it in the shops. She truly has a unique talent.

'Well, what do you think?'

'It is so cute, I almost wish Sorab was a girl.'

Billie smiles. 'You got time for a pot of tea?'

'I do,' I say. She puts the kettle on and we sit and talk. We never mention Blake. Until four thirty when I kiss Sorab and walk out of our front door. Tom gets out of the car and opens the back door when he sees me come down the stairs. I look up and Billie is standing at the balcony looking down at me. She shifts the baby to one hand and waves. I wave back, a feeling of dread in my stomach.

I do not let Tom carry my bags for me or take me upstairs. I know the way. Besides, I am dying to be alone with just my chaotic thoughts. I go through the glass door and Mr. Nair leaps to his feet from his position behind the reception counter like a startled meerkat. He comes towards me beaming.

'Miss Bloom, Miss Bloom,' he cries. 'You are back in the penthouse. I saw all the cleaners and bags and new furniture going upstairs and I wondered who it would be.'

'How nice to see you again, Mr. Nair.'

He holds out his hands. 'Here, let me help you with your bags.'

I pull the bags out of his reach. 'It's OK, Mr. Nair. They are very light. I can manage. Why don't you come up tomorrow morning for a coffee instead, and we can have a nice chat, then.'

'Oh yes, Miss Bloom. That will be wonderful. It hasn't been the same ever since you left.'

I smile. In truth I too have missed him and his fantastic stories of an India gone by. 'I'll call down tomorrow.'

'Goodnight, Miss Bloom. It really is good to have you back.'

I bid him goodnight, enter the lift and slip my key card into its slot. The doors swish close and I am borne up. Strange, I never thought I would be coming back here again and yet here I am. The doors open and it is all the same. Nothing, but nothing has changed.

I unlock the front door and open it. The same faint fragrance of lilies that I always associate with this apartment wafts out. Such a feeling of nostalgia rushes over me that I feel my knees go weak. I close the door, put my packages on the side table, and walk down that long enameled corridor. I run my fingers along the cool smooth wall the way I had done more than a year ago.

I don't go into the living room, but turn off and go into the bedroom. A sob rises in my throat. Nothing has changed even here. It is as if I was here yesterday and not more than a year ago. I go into the room next to it and, as Laura promised, it has been set up to function as a nursery. There is a beautiful white and blue cot, all kinds of toys, a very swanky-looking pram and tins of baby formula. I go to them. I recognize them. I have seen them advertised, all natural and made of goat's milk, but I could not afford them. I pick one up and look at it and experience a shaft of guilt.

I have denied Sorab all this. Am I really doing the right thing by him? Will he thank me one day for depriving him of a life that 99.99 percent of people can only dream of? The answer is confusing and I don't want to go there. I know I will go there, it is too important not to, but not yet. Not today. It is already six o'clock.

I close the door and go into the bathroom and switch

on the lights. In the immaculate space I am a stranger with a beautiful hairdo. I stare at myself. The night stretches out in front of me. I am excited and fearful of what it will bring. I sit on the toilet seat for a moment to compose myself.

I take my dress out of the exclusive-looking bag Rêgine packed it in and hang it up in the bedroom. Then I run a bath, add lavender oil, step into it, and, lying back, close my eyes, but I am too nervous and excited to relax and after a few minutes I get out and, wrapping myself in a fluffy bathrobe that smells of squashed berries, I go into the kitchen.

In the fridge there I find two bottles of champagne lying on their sides. I remember the last time when I stood in the balcony and drank to my mother's health. This time champagne doesn't seem appropriate. I close the door restlessly and go to the liquor cabinet. There I pour myself a very large shot of vodka. Standing by the bar I knock it back. It runs like fire into my empty stomach, but it has the desired effect of almost immediately settling my nerves. I look at my hands. They have stopped shaking.

I go back into the bathroom and carefully apply my make-up. Two layers of mascara, a touch of blusher, and nude lip gloss. I move away from the mirror.

'Not bad, Bloom. Good job.'

I go back to the alcohol counter and pour myself another large vodka, down it and, feeling decidedly light-headed and, devil may care, go to the bedroom. I take my beautiful white dress off the hanger and change into it. As I gently ease it over my head a hook catches on my hair and pulls a lock out of place. I stare in horror at the dangling lock. Cursing, I try to twist it and push it back into place. My efforts are somewhat successful and I sigh with relief. I zip up and step into my shoes and look at myself in the mirror.

A sophisticated woman with glittering eyes and high color stares back. Too much blusher. With cotton wool I remove it all. The heat and the alcohol have tinged my cheeks pink. No need for blusher. I dab my finger with perfume and touch it behind my ears.

There I am, ready for the great Barrington.

Eight

I kill ten minutes pacing the balcony tiles in my Cinderella shoes. At 8:05 exactly Tom rings the bell. His eyes widen when I open the door.

'That's a beautiful outfit, Miss Bloom,' he says, with an embarrassed cough. He is holding a long cardboard box, which he awkwardly slips onto the side-table. I look at it and feel the color rush up my neck. Oh my God! Blake really means for this to be a re-creation of our first night together.

As the lift descends I already know where Tom is taking me.

Madame Yula is filled with the same sort of people that had populated it the last time I was there. If this is a re-creation of our first night together then I know exactly where I will find Blake. Waiting at the bar. I turn towards it and even though I know what I will see, my heart stops. He is wearing a charcoal suit, black shirt and a white tie, and he is the most beautiful man in the place…but that is not it… I am being eaten alive by his eyes. For a long moment I stand frozen, simply caught and staring back at the *hunger* in his stormy blue eyes. It is so naked and raw it shocks me.

'Mademoiselle,' someone says, close to my ear. I turn in the direction of the voice, my expression blank, distracted, perhaps even confused. 'Can I help you?' the waiter queries.

Before I can answer, Blake is there.

'She's with me,' he says smoothly, and the waiter slips away, the way waiters in movies do. I turn my head and look up into Blake's face. In the glow of candles and soft lighting he seems dark and impossibly mysterious. For a moment neither of us speaks. We never broke up. It's all there crackling between us. The sex-rumpled sheets, the slim hips wrapped only in a towel, the hungry mouth, and the hours upon hours of fucking. I shiver with the memories. My lips part. An invitation that cannot be missed.

But a shutter comes over his eyes.

'How complete is the illusion that beauty is goodness,' he murmurs.

Vaguely it registers that it is quotation, but my stunned brain cannot locate the source. A hand reaches out to take that escaped lock of hair that has worked free of my efforts to keep it up. Gently he twirls the strands in his fingers and carefully reinserts them into place. His hand drops off.

'Would you like a drink?'

It occurs to me that I am already a little drunk. 'No, I had some back at the flat.'

His eyes flash. 'Champagne.' He remembered.

I shake my head. 'Vodka.'

He nods. 'Food for you then,' he says.

We are shown to the same table. I look closely at him. Try to see beyond the mask, but his face is deliberately blank. In a daze I order food. It arrives. I pick up my knife and fork. Slip it between my lips. Taste nothing. I lift my eyes to him and catch him watching me. His eyes are ravenous. His food untouched. Between my legs I ache. I swallow the food in my mouth. It becomes a lump that sticks in my throat. I reach for the wine glass and take a gulp, but that only makes me choke. I start to cough. My eyes fill with water. Fuck. Trust me to do something so sexually unappealing.

'Are you all right?'

'Fine,' I say flushing with embarrassment. I need to go to the Ladies and sort myself out.

'Excuse me,' I croak, putting the napkin on the table and standing up.

He stands when I do. I leave the table and feel his eyes boring into me until I round the bend. I go into the Ladies and look at myself in the mirror. And again I am surprised by my reflection. I honestly can hardly recognize myself, the new hairstyle, the clothes, the make-up, but more than all of that is the look in my eyes.

Wild. 'I am Lana from the council estate, mother of Sorab,' I say aloud.

That piece of hair comes loose again. I carefully pull one of the pins out a little and wind the hair around that pin. It seems to do the job. I take a deep breath and go back out to the restaurant.

While I have been away Blake has not touched his food. Instead, he has finished his whiskey and ordered another. He looks at me from above the rim of his glass.

'Aren't you hungry?' I ask.

He puts his glass down and catches my fingers. His hands are exactly as I remember, firm, warm, strong. He turns them over and looks at my nails.

'Very nice,' he says softly, and bringing them to his lips kisses them. It is a mocking gesture, but at the touch of his cool lips I tremble with anticipation. I remember them smiling with sexual invitation. He lets his fingers run up the skin of my wrist. 'Pure fucking silk.' His eyes rise up to meet mine. Between the thick lashes they are potent, compelling. 'Have you missed me even a little, Lana?'

For an instant, I forget myself and respond to the emotion I see simmering in his eyes. 'There is not a day that has gone by where I have not longed for you,' I whisper.

As if I have slapped him, he snatches his hand away and begins to laugh bitterly. He shakes his head as if in wonder. 'I see now why I was fooled by you. You're downright lethal. A very, very dangerous seductress indeed I have caught in my net.'

He drains his glass and, looking away from me, gestures to a waiter for another. When he turns back to face me, his eyes are glittering. 'So how much did my father pay you?'

I pause. I am in dangerous territory. My contract with Victoria does not allow me to reveal the sum or even tell anyone that I have been paid by her. The waiter arrives with his whiskey and sets it down in front of him.

'Another,' Blake barks.

The waiter nods discreetly and clears his empty glass in one smooth movement. Blake does not take his eyes off me.

Billie is right. My position is untenable. In his eyes I must be the worst kind of slut. Ahead lies only more misunderstanding and pain for both of us. The pain has already begun, a physical ache. It fills my chest. I can never tell him the truth. In his mind I will always be his bad romance. Lady Gaga singing, 'I want your ugly. I want your disease.'

'I'm sorry, but I had to sign a non-disclosure agreement,' I say, with the full knowledge that without the truth he will always despise me. I lean back in my chair feeling soiled. I will never again be clean in his eyes. And there is not a damn thing I can do about it. The waiter returns with more whiskey.

'I know you're angry but—'

'Shut the fuck up. You have no idea,' he grates through gritted teeth.

I close my mouth. I have never seen him so openly angry. He is always so controlled, so smooth. Even when he was once angry with someone on the phone his fury was so tightly leashed, so frighteningly quiet that I stood stock still behind the door listening.

He shoots his whiskey aggressively, and turning the empty glass on its edge rolls it on the tablecloth. 'Do you want more food?'

I shake my head miserably. This is turning out to be nothing like I imagined.

A muscle in his jaw twitches. He calls for the bill.

Someone in a suit comes rushing to his side. 'Is anything the matter?' he enquires worriedly.

'Everything is fine.' He looks at me hard and deep.

'But your main course...'

Blake does not take his eyes off me. 'I have unfinished business to take care of, Anton.'

I flush badly and Anton slips away with impressive speed from that which has nothing to do with him. Another waiter, his face schooled into impassive professionalism, comes bearing the bill. Blake signs for it, unfolds himself out of his chair and comes to stand by me. I get to my feet and he leads me out of the restaurant. We do not touch except for his hand splayed on the small of my back. Possessive, the way only a husband's hand should be.

Not a word is spoken by either of us in the car, but every cell in my body is responding to his nearness. My desire for him is such that my hands are clenched tight against my thighs and my sex is actually throbbing. In fact, the need is so excessive it is almost violent. I sneak a look at him. He is staring ahead, the chiseled cheekbones like stone, but that muscle in his throat is ticking like a time bomb. I know that tick. It tells me what he cannot, how hard and deep he wants to fuck me. He is well and truly snared inside his bad romance.

'What happened to all the clothes I left behind?' I ask in the lift.

'You enquire about last season's fashions? What about the people you left behind, Lana? Why don't you enquire about them? Me for instance.'

'How have you been, Blake?'

'You're just about to find out,' he replies with a nasty grin.

Nine

I hear the soft, thick click of the door behind me, and turn around to face him. He stands there, tall, dark and throbbing with sexual tension. God! How I want this man. A rough sound rumbles in his throat. I recognize it. Blind, earth-shattering desire. It has been a long time since I heard it. Makes me rock on my feet. He shoots out a hand and pulls me hard towards him. My body slams into his.

I have the impression of stone—unmoving. It will break, but it will never bend. But I can bend. I mold my hips into his. His erection is thick and hot against my stomach. The rawness of it awakens that great beast inside me. Greedy, relentless thing. It wants more, it wants it all, and it wants it right now. Intoxicated by the smoldering fire in his eyes my hands snake up his chest and twine around his neck, but his strong hands come up and untangle mine. He catches them in his and takes them behind my back. His clasp is a firm handcuff.

Very deliberately he holds me away from him and lets his half-lidded eyes rove my parted mouth, my breasts—thrust out towards him and heaving, down my body, to my legs. His eyes lift again to meet mine. I am impossibly aroused.

'I had half a dozen fantasies of what I wanted to do to you when I got you naked. Tame sex is not one of them,' he says, as he plucks out the pins in my hair and flings them away. Released, my hair falls all around my face and shoulders.

'My beautiful whore. Once I was good to you and you kicked me when I was down; now you get what you deserve.'

Without warning he grips the two sides of the high collar of my lovely dress and rips it into two. I clutch the torn ends of my ruined dress together and stare at him in shock.

He looks down at me, breathing hard. Strangely, he is as cold as ice. My mind is in unbelievable chaos. I have misjudged the extent of his fury. Underneath the façade of calm he is seething with anger at what he perceives to be my duplicity. I want to cry at the wanton destruction of something so beautiful, but in fact I am too shocked to cry.

'Dress only in what's in the box and meet me in the bedroom,' he commands curtly, and walks away from me.

I stand there a little longer, too dazed to move. I

glimpsed the fierce hunger, and need; now all I see is the iron control in his tense shoulders. He stops in front of the bar and pours himself a whiskey. I pick up the box by the side table and go to the bathroom.

Quickly, I take off the torn dress and stuff it into the chrome bin under the sink. As the lid closes over it a sob escapes my lips. I had never owned anything so fine before. It had suggested curves where there were jutting bones and made me feel so elegant and sophisticated. I could still see Fleur grinning with delight and Madame Règine rasping, 'One of a kind. You will not find another like it.'

I press my hand to my mouth and avoid my reflection. I will not cry. I will be strong, I tell myself while, another part of me stands appalled by his violence. I know what is in the box. I pull the satin ribbons and lift the cover of the box.

And frown.

It is not white lingerie and shoes.

As if in a trance, I pick up the familiar velvet box and open it. Under the yellow lights of the bathroom the diamonds in the sapphire necklace glitter like the bling on a rap singer. The next thing I find in the box is even more surprising. Billie's shorts, the ones I borrowed to wear to the party. I must have left them behind. I had totally forgotten them. I remember that night again. What did it mean? That he himself has gone through all my stuff and kept these? That this item of clothing means something to him? I open the last item—a shoe box. A pair of snake skin orange Christian Louboutin shoes, but startlingly similar to the ones I wore the first night we met.

I try to imagine how he came upon them. Did he describe them to Laura? Did she then search the net and give him a list to choose from? I undress quickly. I consider leaving my knickers on, but I remember his eyes when he held my hands behind my back and told me everything I should be wearing is in the box.

The necklace is cold on my skin. I pull the shorts on, zip and button them. I get into the shoes and look at myself in the mirror. Oh dear. The shorts hang about my hip bones and my rib bones show. I look gawky and awkward and as sexy as a pole in shorts. I console myself that the lights in the bedroom will be muted. I stare at my breasts. The nipples are erect. This morning I could have covered them with my hair, but now that the front has been feathered that option is gone.

I touch the light switch and kill the light, in the hope that he will not see the silhouette of my skinny frame, or my half-naked exit from the bathroom. My steps falter and I stand uncertainly by the wall in my high heels. Half-hidden in the shadows at the edges of the room, I stand and stare at the magnificent specimen sitting shirtless, in a pool of light on the bed.

His legs are crossed at the ankles and his arms are folded across his chest. The muscles of his arms seem even more defined than I remember. He must have taken his frustrations out in the gym. He moves slightly and the action ripples the golden row of thick muscles in his stomach. My mouth dries. Suddenly I feel exposed and ashamed of my body, my arousal. My hands rise up to cover my breasts. My nipples are hard pebbles against the palms of my hands.

'Come in,' he purrs. His voice is silk, but his eyes are shadowed and his face is a blank wall. Expressionless. Impenetrable.

He begins to unbutton his trousers. I stare at the flat stomach, the beautiful body that I have longed for. The trousers slip to the floor. Black briefs. The bulge is clearly, clearly visible. Dear me, but it's been so long. I feel my own body producing its juices, getting ready for the sweet invasion. He steps out of his briefs. Wow! Nothing has changed. He is as gorgeous as ever.

But I don't move. I can't. My soul refuses to allow me to go forward. Not towards that demeaning drill again. I remember it like yesterday. Go to the middle of the room, strip, turn around, spread my legs as wide as they will go, and bend down to touch the floor. Then it had been strangely exciting, but now it seems sordid. I'm not here because he paid me to be here. I'm here willingly. I am here to atone for a wrong I did him. I'm here because, even though he doesn't believe it, I'm crazy in love with him.

'New games, Lana?' he mocks when I make no move towards him, but his voice is different. The silk is gone. It is sinuous and alive with the kind of unthinking lust that only a man knows how to feel.

I watch him bound off the bed, and come towards me, tall, dark, dangerous, and looking for trouble. He stops in front of me. Heat comes off his body in waves. The air thickens. I want to taste that golden skin. I blink to break the spell. *Take control, Lana.* The blackness of what I have made him become envelops me like a bleak shadow. His vengeful eyes bore into me.

A strange fascination with danger slides down my spine. I want to shut my eyes and try to picture him as he was, but I don't. One wrong move and he'll take me now, roughly, and the chasm between us will become wider, impossible to breach. But a woman is never without options, my mother always said. Start the way you mean to carry on. I need not be powerless. I can be as powerful as Billie, as powerful as my mother.

I take my hands away from my breasts and slip the copper button of my shorts out of its eye. Slowly I unzip my shorts. His eyes do not follow my fingers but watch my face. Even so my fingers are trembling with a kind of feral excitement. I don't have to push them down my legs. They are so loose they run down like water. For a while I stand there in my necklace and my high shoes.

When I lift one leg to step out of the shorts, he catches my leg firmly under the knee and forces it up high so I am spread open to him. I feel air in places that have never seen the sun. My gesture of submission has done nothing to lessen his cold regard. His eyes are deliberately barren. I wonder how someone can be as turned on as he obviously is and still look so cold and distant.

His other hand cups one bare buttock possessively and my pussy, already wet, floods and clenches with anticipation. He plays with the wetness he has aroused. Pleasure and delicious release shimmer between us. It has been so long. My body doesn't care how he does it or why he wants to do it. It just wants him inside. It has always been like that for me. My body weeping for him. He lets his fingers sweep along my open sex and brings it to his mouth. He sucks his fingers.

'Mmnnn you still taste like heaven.'

I whimper and that sound has an electrifying effect on him. With a growl he thrusts his fingers into me. Again. And again. Harder. Faster. A sound escapes my lips. My head presses against the wall and my hips thrust towards his hand. He is rough, but after all this time I welcome it. My pussy creams with the force. I feel the excess fluid trickle down my thighs.

But it is not enough.

I rock my hips mindlessly. Looking to fill that ache. Where his fingers cannot reach. Begging him with my body, with every jerk and every gasp, but he will not give me that. His fingers pump with a steady, forceful tempo, pushing me towards a rough, humiliating climax.

Which comes while I am standing on one foot like a stork, my body twisted open. The rapture is explosive. My muscles lose all their strength and I sag against the wall behind me. The dizzying roar of my own blood abates to a dull thud. He looks at me with frosty eyes.

He wants me to lower my head in shame while he pretends he has felt nothing. But I know different. My eyes defiant, I lift a hand and cup his hard erection.

'You are as aroused as I am.'

He smiles. 'Sure,' he drawls. 'I want to fuck you. What man wouldn't? To tell you the truth, babe, I'm drowning in lust.'

He lets go of my leg and with rough hands grabs me by the upper arms, whirls me around, and pushes me forward. My palms and forearms hit the wall. My right cheek is pressed against the cold surface of the wall and my breasts are crushed into it. He takes the hair that covers my face from his gaze and hooks it behind my ear. He wants to watch me. My eyes swivel desperately to the side to look at him, but I cannot see him.

"You taste and smell the same, let's see if you feel the same,' he says, and, lifting me slightly off the ground, grasps my thighs and spreads them wide apart. My shoes fall off with a dull thud. He returns my bare feet to the ground soundlessly. His large hands grab my hips and tilt my lower body so it is perfectly aligned with his cockhead. For a second I feel him tease me by running it along my clit and then he drives into me.

The impact makes me shudder and my breath catch in my throat. My mouth opens in a soundless cry. I draw a breath quickly. Prepare myself for the next swift thrust of pleasure. It comes before I am ready. This time I cannot help it, I utter a strange cry, but my muscles are already clenching him and sucking him even deeper into my body.

He sets up a rapid pace. Every wild plunge into my depths has me jerking in response. Slowly I am lifted higher and higher until I am standing uncomfortably on the tips of my toes, my hips tilting higher and higher, wanting more and more of the gloriously thick invasion. My thighs and calf muscles are so tense they start to ache and my heart is beating so fast I feel it thudding like a drum inside my ribcage. My sex becomes a greedy, hungry mouth sucking at him.

I force myself to hold my body in the same position while he hammers into me until, with one last painful thrust that I register at the base of my womb, he calls my name and finds his climax. His cum is slick and hot inside me. For a second his nose nuzzles in the crook of my neck and then he rouses himself and pushes away from me.

I don't turn to face him, but slowly set my heels down to the ground and push myself away from the wall. I will gather myself a tiny bit more before I turn again to face his condemnation. I feel weak, raw, bruised, abused, vulnerable, but...satisfied. I should have felt shame, but I don't. I love this man.

I turn around slowly.

He is dressing quickly. While buttoning his shirt with his back to me, he says, 'I will get Laura to send you a morning after pill.'

A stray thought. *A bit late for that, mate.* If he knew. If he only knew. I say nothing, suddenly feeling my nakedness. Soon he will be dressed and I will be the only naked one in the room. I begin to walk to the bathroom.

'Wait,' he orders. I long to cover myself, but I do not. He cannot humiliate me. I will not allow it.

When he is fully dressed he turns and looks at my exposed body. It is masked well, but it is still there, the hunger. Still now. When he has just been satiated. So much remains that my eyes widen. It is the same for me: I want him again. I am just as helpless to the call of his body.

But he turns away from me.

I watch him go to the side cupboard and pull out a book. It is covered in leather. Looks like a journal. He tosses it on the bed next to me. 'This is for you. I want you to keep a record of everything I do to you.'

'Why?' I whisper.

'For my reading pleasure?'

'That's just sick. I'm not doing it,' I say.

As if I am a life-size doll he picks me up and tosses me on the bed. I land on my back with a bounce, but I stare up at him defiantly.

He stands over me. His face is hard and forbidding. Very gently he touches the necklace.

'You're nothing but skin and bone,' he says, almost to himself. His hands reach for my ankles and lifting them up he opens my legs into a V. Turning his head to one side he kisses my right ankle and runs his hot, velvety tongue along my calf. My breathing quickens. At my knee he stops and sucks the tender skin at the back of it, and then that cunning tongue licks on to my inner thigh.

'How much do you want me to taste you?' he whispers.

As an answer I moan and try to push my sticky legs further apart.

'No, ask me nicely.'

'Yes, please,' I beg.

'Please what?' he asks enjoying his dominance and control. His finger lightly circles my wet opening.

'Oh God...please, please... Taste me,' I beg shamelessly.

'Will you write your journal?'

'Yes, yes, I will.'

He straightens his arms and holding my trembling legs open wide he looks at my sex, swollen and drenched with both our juices, a glistening treasure.

'Cunt,' he dismisses, and letting go of my legs leaves the bedroom.

I had heard him tell Tom to wait downstairs, so I knew he was not going to stay the night, but I still flinch when I hear the front door shut. I cup myself between my legs. Slick and sore and unsatisfied. I want more.

Ten

That night I dream of my mother. In my dream we are in a shop. It is very similar to Madame Rêgine's boutique, but it is full of wedding dresses. My mother points to a long dress that is ripped in half. 'That's perfect for you,' she says.

'But it's torn,' I say.

'That's how Victoria likes it,' she says sadly.

I wake up disturbed and unhappy. I have never spent a night away from Sorab and I miss him terribly. It is four in the morning and it is dark outside. I get dressed in the jeans and T-shirt that I arrived in and leave the apartment. I exit the lift and the night porter nods at me. I return the gesture and open the doors.

The air outside is crisp and fresh. I walk along the side of the block, cross the road and enter the park. Then I begin to run. There is no one else around and I run until I am breathless and so weary I can barely walk.

Then I stumble onto a park bench and watch the sun come up. My thoughts are jumbled. I refuse to put them in order. I am actually afraid of them. Afraid of the future.

A man and his German shepherd come into the park. It is off the lead and it runs at great speed up to me.

'Don't be afraid,' he shouts. 'She won't harm you. She's just a puppy. She wants to be friends.'

She jumps up on my knees and starts licking my face. Her exuberance is such that I break out in laughter. Oh, if only life were so simple. I look into her gold-brown eyes and run my fingers through her silky coat feeling the wild life that is coursing through her body. In contrast, I feel drained and jaded. As if I am a husk left on the mill floor. After a while the man whistles and she bounds away, but the exchange has left me lifted as I walk back to the apartment. The night porter is getting ready to go home. Soon Mr. Nair's shift will begin.

I stand in the shower for ages. When I come out my mobile is double blinking. Fleur has left a message that two racks of clothes, shoes, and accessories will be arriving at 10:00 am. I am to choose whatever I want and somebody will come and pick up anything I don't want at 5:00 pm. I am to call her if I need any help. I text back to thank her. Then I text Billie.

Are you awake?

Billie calls back. 'Hey.'

'Oh good, you're awake,' I say, happy to hear her voice.

'Yeah, the little monster got me up early.'

'Is he all right?'

'Shouldn't you be asking *me* if I'm all right?'

I laugh guiltily. 'Hey, you want to come around about tenish. Fleur is sending some clothes for me to try on. You can help me decide which to keep.'

'That'll be fun.'

'I'll call a minicab for you for ten.'

'Got to go. The creature has just started wailing again,' she says. 'But see ya tenish.' I hear Sorab's cries in the background just before she terminates the call and feel a sharp pang of loss. That should have been me. That's my life. Not stuck all alone in an empty apartment. I know that Billie is enjoying her time with Sorab. With her, true affection is masked by insults. Hello, Repulsive, she will say to her lover. I realize that I already miss him too much. Maybe tomorrow I will tell Blake it is my turn to babysit Sorab. And have him with me for two days.

At nine thirty I invite Mr. Nair up for a coffee. He comes through the door holding his *I'm the Boss* mug, his eyes bulging with curiosity.

We sit at the kitchen counter. 'What happened to you, Miss Bloom?' he asks.

'I had to go to Iran suddenly.'

'Oh! No wonder. Poor Mr. Barrington. You broke his heart,' he states, enlarging his eyes dramatically. I watch him bite into a biscuit. Crumbs land on his jacket. I look at them, but my mind is spinning.

'Why do you say that?' I ask as casually as I can manage.

'Because,' he says, 'I was the one who gave him your letter.'

'My letter?'

'Yes. Have you forgotten, you sent your friend with a note instructing the porter on duty to give the envelope to Mr. Barrington? It was a strange note, very formal, not at all like you, but I knew it was you because I always recognize your handwriting.'

I take a sip of coffee, swallow and lick my lips. 'What did Mr. Barrington say when you gave it to him?'

'I tell you, Miss Bloom, it was the oddest thing. He practically snatched it out of my hand, tore it open and read it right in front of me. The contents shocked him so very much I saw his eyes go back to the top of the letter to read it again. Then he crushed the letter in his hand and walked out of this building...and I have never seen him since.'

I bite my lip. The past. I can never change it, but then would I? How can I regret it? Sorab came out of my sorry past.

Mr. Nair pops the last bit of biscuit into his mouth and hops nimbly off the stool. 'My ten minutes are up. I'd better go.'

'My friend Billie will be coming this morning. Will you call me to let me know when she does?'

'I can do better than that, Miss Bloom. I will show her up myself.'

I thank him and close the door.

An hour after the stuff that Fleur sent arrives Billie breezes in with Mr. Nair in tow.

'Thanks, Mr. Nair,' I say relieving him of a large bag of baby things.

'I'm very happy to help you, Miss Bloom.' He nods happily towards Sorab. 'He looks exactly like his father. A very handsome boy, indeed.'

I freeze.

But Billie is quick off the mark. She grins broadly. 'Sorry, mate, but this one here is my baby. Don't you think he looks like me? Everyone says so.'

Mr. Nair's dark, confused eyes look to me.

'I'm only his godmother,' I say weakly, filled with a sharp sense of pain. I am terribly proud of Sorab, and not being recognized as his mother is far more difficult than I expected.

'Oh, I'm very, very sorry. I spoke out of turn,' Mr. Nair apologizes. Poor man. He looks embarrassed and flustered.

'Please don't worry about it, Mr. Nair. I know you meant no harm.'

'Better be going. The desk is unmanned,' Mr. Nair mutters awkwardly and hurries away.

I close the door and turn towards Billie. 'Oh my God, Billie. He knew.'

'Of course he did. He is Indian. They are into astrology and all that shit, aren't they?'

'Billie,' I wail. 'Recognizing a family resemblance has nothing to do with astrology.'

Billie crosses her arms. 'I know that! I was being sarcastic. For God's sake, Lana, what's got into you? Sorab is a three-month-old baby and *all* babies look alike. I wouldn't even be able to pick him out from a line-up of six babies.'

I frown unconvinced. I believe that Sorab is one of those children who have very definite features. 'He *does* have his father's eyes.'

'Look, you said Blake's secretary sent a whole list of baby stuff, including pram and cot, to the apartment, right? So he's obviously seen it all go into the lift, put two and two together and come up with four. Unfortunately for him, the correct answer is five. Now, quit fretting over things you don't need to worry about and give me a tour of this awesome flat.'

I smile. I am such a paranoid fool. Of course, she is right. I give her a grand tour.

'Wow!' she enthuses. 'Guess how much this crib costs?'

'I don't know. Five hundred quid?'

'Add another zero and you're almost there.'

'Really?'

She pulls the price tag off and holds it out to me. 'Five thousand five hundred and fifty-nine pounds for a fucking crib when a third of the world is starving.' She shakes her head. 'Still it is dead cool to be so stonkingly rich, isn't it?'

My phone rings. It is Laura. She is calling to tell me that Tom is on his way with my morning after pill and to tell me to be ready for 8:00 pm. She has made a dinner reservation for Blake and me at The Fat Duck.

'It sure looks good from the outside, though,' Billie says, having listened to my conversation with Laura.

Billie finds a box of chocolates in the kitchen and then lunges headlong into the bed and, lying sprawled on it like a sultan, makes me try all the clothes on, one by one. She insists I keep a pair of pink leather pants. 'You got to. They make your bum look all ripe and trapped and in need of saving. Blake is an ass man, right?'

'How do you know?'

'Just a guess. Now go try on the long black dress,' she orders.

The black dress makes her gasp. 'Very, very sexy.'

I grin.

'How many are you allowed to keep?'

'As many as I want, I think.'

'Really? What's that like?'

For some reason I think of the white dress. 'Nice, I guess.'

'What happened last night?'

'He's angry with me, Bill. Very angry.'

'He didn't hurt you, did he?' I can hear the protective anger come into Billie's voice. She is such a firebrand.

'No,' I say, but I find it almost impossible to discuss how I feel about Blake with Billie. For Billie sex is fun, something to do when she feels horny. For me, and I suspect for Blake as well, it is a clawing need. I know it is the reason why he is angry. He hates losing control. Control is important to him. In fact, if I am given only one word to describe his personality, I would have to use the word controlled. His whole life is about control of himself and others. He is controlled in everything he does, what he eats, how he eats, all his dealings, the precision of his time keeping, his immaculate appearance. I don't think I have ever seen a single scuff mark on his shoes.

Until I came everything was perfectly in order, compartmentalized. There was room for a fiancée and a mistress. Now it is all a mess. I am like the lock of hair on his head that will not be tamed. He wants to walk away and feel nothing but disgust for me, but he can't. I look Billie in the eye.

'His real anger is not directed at me, but at himself for still wanting me.'

'I've no beef with him. I only fear it will all blow up and he will not be able or willing to protect you against his family and the bitch.'

I do not tell her about my near run-in with Victoria in Harvey Nichols. That would be putting the cat among the pigeons. She stays until the five o'clock rush hour traffic abates at six. I send her home with a heavy heart and a couple of tins of the goat's milk formula.

At seven I come out of the bath and slip into a blue dress. It is long and straight with a demure neckline, but it dramatically deepens the blue of my eyes and suggests the curves that I no longer possess. I am stepping into a pair of peacock blue shoes when I hear him come in. I look at my watch. He is early. I turn in surprise when he comes directly into the bedroom. For a moment we look at each other. He is wearing a silver-gray suit, a white shirt, and a black and red striped tie.

'I hope you haven't dressed in a nun's habit on my account, because it is coming off the first chance I get,' he says.

Once he might have come up to me and told me how beautiful I looked. My hands flutter upwards uselessly and settle down to my sides. Now he will not accept anything except that which suggests I am a slut. He goes towards the bed. The journal is lying on the bedside table. He picks it up and opens it to the empty first page. He comes towards me expressionless. He reaches a hand into his jacket and emerges with a sleek black fountain pen. Swiss. Very expensive. He holds the journal and the pen wordlessly out to me.

I take the offered items and go into the dining room. I sit at the long, polished table and write.

Day 1

Blake ripped the first dress that I have actually loved into two and fucked me hard against the bedroom wall. Then he threw me on the bed, didn't deliver on his promise, and used the C word on me.

I go back into the living room where Blake is pouring himself a shot of whiskey so large my eyes actually widen. I hand him the book and his pen. He opens the book, reads the two sentences I have written and looks at me with amusement.

'The C word. May I remind you that you come from a council estate where the…er…C word is almost an adjective?'

I lift my chin. 'I first heard that word in the playground when I was six years old. A mother had sat on one of the benches by the swings and described her toddler daughter as a 'clever little cunt'. So I came home and used the word in front of my mother. She didn't scold me or wash my mouth out with soap. "I have obviously failed in my duty as a mother that you feel comfortable to allow such a vile word to sit on your tongue. I will not eat until I realize where I have gone wrong," she said. She put dinner on the table and refused to eat. "Of course you have to eat. You have done nothing wrong," she told me. I had to sit there and finish all my food. She would not let me leave a single pea behind. She did it again at breakfast. By lunchtime I was so distraught I could not eat a single mouthful. I promised her I would never use the word again. And I haven't until today.'

He steps away from me, as if knowing that little bit about me is poisonous to his sanity or well-being. 'If you are ready we should leave now.'

Outside he remote unlocks a white Lamborghini. The wings lift upwards. It is the kind of flashy car I associate with the spoilt sons of Saudi Arabian oil sheiks. I settle in. 'What happened to Aston?'

'Wrapped it around a tree.'

I swing my head around. 'With you in it?'

'Yes, cracked a couple of ribs, but, as you can see, I emerged unscathed. It's hard to hurt me.'

There is an edge to his voice. Of course. He is telling me I have hurt him.

The Fat Duck is the same as I remember it. Great service and divine food, but there is a large difference that I cannot not notice. Blake is drinking far more than he used to. He orders the obligatory bottle of wine that perfectly matches our meal, but hardly touches it. Instead, he goes for the whiskey. I have already counted seven.

'You were completely drunk when you had your accident, weren't you?'

'Yup. Miss Marple solves yet another mystery.'

'Didn't they do you?'

The alcohol has relaxed his tense shoulders somewhat. He laughs and I want to press my mouth against those hard lips. 'Have you forgotten everything I told you, Lana dear? The Barringtons are above the law. Cream always floats to the top.'

'So does shit.'

He raises his glass and chuckles without mirth. 'Let's see how bright you can be when you are naked in my bed.'

'Depends how full my mouth will be,' I retort unwisely.

'To bursting, darling.'

I feel my cheeks heat up. 'Are you planning to drive home tonight?'

He picks up his glass and shoots it. 'I wouldn't risk your pretty face on my windshield for anything. Tom is coming to pick us up.'

In the car we do not touch each other. Our conversation is stilted and shallow, unsustainable.

What did you do today?

Billie came around with her baby.

Fun?

Yes.

Both of us are already thinking of the time we will be alone. When only our bodies will speak. There is something about this man that makes my hands itch to touch his skin, suck that firm mouth, meld with him... forever. Desire fogs my brain.

I pretend to drop my purse. He bends to retrieve it, but I reach out for it and brush his clothed thigh. Immediately I feel him tense.

'Don't push me, Lana. I am already on the edge,' he

warns.

We are like tinder and kindling.

Eleven

In the lift I raise my eyes to meet his.

Fuck. What the hell?

The door whooshes open.

He takes my hand and drags me behind him. Opens the door and pulls me through, and leaning back against it tugs me to him so I fall smack onto him. My purse finds a quick path to the carpet, opens its guts, spills. His hot mouth finds mine. The kiss is rough, crazy intense, and full of urgent need. It is what I saw in his eyes. I go astray. I don't want to come back from this. His hand locates the zip at the back of my neck. That hapless zip flies down and the nun's habit pools around my shoes.

His hands expertly release the clasp on my bra. One tug and it is gone the way of the dress. I am so lost in the jaws of desire that I barely hear the sound of light lace tearing. Once again, I am naked and he is fully dressed.

For a moment he holds me at arm's length simply looking at me, the way he used to do in the beginning. Then he takes me to the gilded mirror on the wall.

'Look at you,' he snarls. 'Your pupils are searching for someone to pleasure you. Anyone would do.'

I want to back away from what I see. My eyes are glazed with lust. I look...hungry, feral...electrified. Yet he is wrong. Anyone would not do.

He strokes my heated cheeks then he bends his head and his strong white teeth nibble at my earlobes. 'Cream and sugar and venom,' he says and bites my neck.

In the mirror my eyes widen with shock and pleasure. The sensation is exquisite. The rush of it makes me feel reckless. He begins to gently suck my skin. I moan. His mouth moves to my nipple. The skilled precision of his mouth starts an aching that travels into my core. I am in a sex-induced frenzy thirsting for him to enter me. The taste of true desire is sweltering. I push my ass into the thick, hard snake between us and yearn for it driving inside me. He puts a finger on my lower lip and lets his finger enter my mouth.

'Suck it.'

I take the finger between my lips and suck it gently at first, and then harder. He starts to unbuckle his belt.

I get on my knees. The carpet digs into my skin. I open his fly, pull up his shirt, and kiss that hard, tight stomach. He becomes very still. My tongue flicks out. Tentative, but not for long. I lick the golden brown skin, find the line of fine hair and follow it all the way to the elasticized band of his shorts. My teeth grasp the material and pull. His cock springs free and hovers, swollen and angry over my mouth. I take the throbbing ready meat in my hand. The head swells, surges, pulses, and comes alive in my hand.

I use both my hands to quickly pull the briefs down his thighs while my mouth takes in that gorgeous, rock-hard cock. I look up at him and watch him draw his breath sharply. Slowly, I move forward and let him witness every inch of his dick sliding between my lips. He pulses in my mouth and that pushes me into sucking greedily at the head of his erection. I devour him, taking him deeper and deeper into my mouth.

He thrusts his hips forward, jamming himself down my throat. It makes me gag, but it still feels right. His cock should always be inside me. It is where it belongs. Anything else would be wrong. I am struck by the potency of my obsession.

'Yes. Yes, like that... Exactly like that.'

He keeps my head in place with his hands as his thrusts become more and more urgent until with rigid muscles and a fierce groan, he buckles, and I feels his hot seed jet to the back of my throat. It is slick and leaves a tang on the back of my tongue as I swallow. He stays in my mouth, his head thrown back for a few moments more. My eyes look up at him, waiting for what I do not know. His face drops down, shadowed, to look at me, my mouth stuffed with his meat.

'Very pretty,' he says softly. 'You were born to suck

dick. I'm surprised I never realized it before.' He pulls out of me. 'Now go and sit on the bed.'

I stand and simply look at him. He wants to humiliate me. It will be a cold day in hell before I allow him to succeed. Naked and barefoot, but head held high I walk to the bedroom. I go up to the bed and as instructed sit on the edge. He appears at the door. Again he is fully clothed and in control while I am naked and defenseless.

'No, with your back against the headboard.'

I scoot up and lean against the plump pillows.

He comes and sits on the bed beside me. His voice is casual, conversational. 'What did you do for sex in the past year?'

I flush.

Some hardness barely leashed has crept into his voice. 'Did you take a lover?'

I shake my head.

'Did you go without?' Curious.

I shake my head again.

'Show me what you did?'

'I can't,' I whisper.

'Show me.' An order.

I open my mouth, but he silences me with a finger on my lips, his head shaking gently. 'You obviously don't understand how this works,' he explains. 'The only words I want to hear pass those delectable lips are yes, please, and more.' He takes his finger off my lips. 'Was it any of those words or a combination of them?'

I shake my head slowly.

'I thought so. Show me,' he says, and now his voice is coldly authoritative.

I press my lips together. I feel that flash of defiance return. That's what he wants. He wants to watch me masturbate in front of him. Fine. Let him see that. He has seen everything else. He folds his arms. Slowly I open my legs. He smiles slightly at my submission. I bring my fingers to my clit and close my eyes.

'Open your eyes.'

My eyes snap open. Locking my gaze with his glittering ones I move a finger into the opening of my sex. The folds are covered in slick juices, and collecting some from the opening I move my fingers around the sensitive nub, slowly teasing it to attention.

His carefully guarded eyes never leave me. 'What did you think of while playing with yourself?'

'You.'

His expression doesn't change, but his eyes flicker. 'Didn't you miss my dick inside you?'

'Very much.'

He makes a small disbelieving sound and reaches over to what had always been his bedside table. He opens the drawer and I am surprised to see it full of sex toys. All of them still in their packaging. I even catch the glimpse of a pair of handcuffs. Rummaging around he finds and fetches a vibrator to our bed. It is black and bright orange and large. Scary large. I close my legs in horror. This has nothing to do with sex. This is him punishing me. Filling me up with a large black and orange object.

Reducing me to a piece of meat. Letting me know I'm nothing to him. My resolution to be strong and my conviction that he can never humiliate me if I don't allow it crumble into dust.

'Don't worry. This won't hurt a bit,' he promises, and switches it on. It makes a whirring sound.

I open my eyes and look at it humming in his hand. 'Don't, Blake. Please don't,' I beg.

'Open your legs.'

I shake my head. 'Please. If you insist on punishing me like this… I'll run away.'

'No you won't. Remember I paid for this. Mine to do with as I please. We had a deal. I give you what you want and you give me what I want. I gave you what you wanted. Now it's your turn to give me what I want. And I want to see this big black and orange machine buried inside that sweet, tight pussy of yours.'

I swallow a lump in my throat and lick my lips. 'Why do we need that when we have your cock?'

'Because,' he explains patiently as if he is talking to a particularly obtuse child, 'you won't always have my cock.'

I look into his eyes. I am looking for the passionate lover I adore, but his eyes are purposely blank. I know I will do anything to bring him back to me. From deep inside me I find the strength. He wants to push that inanimate object into me. Let's give him what he wants and see what comes up. Let's see how he fares!

'All right,' I say and open my legs wide.

If he is surprised by my defiant submission he does not let it show. He lets the vibrator touch my clit. I jump.

'Too sensitive?' he queries softly, and moves it slightly away.

He runs the vibrating tip along the wet folds, and very slowly while watching my face he inserts it into me. While I gasp with shock at its size he pushes it into me up to the hilt.'

'Good?' he asks.

'Good,' I reply, my chin lifted, my eyes widened, my fingers grasping the silk duvet underneath.

So he fucks me with it and even though I beg him not to look at me as I crack apart, he stares at me possessively as I come.

Then he gets up and leaves me.

I lay there spread-eagled with the vibrator still inside me staring at the ceiling. The gadget makes a soft muffled sound that I have not noticed during my humiliation. I want to pull it out of me, but my limbs feel like lead. I am in love with him and he just hates me. If he had cared anything for me I would have seen in his eyes, but nothing! I finally understand. I am just a demon that must be exorcised before he marries the daughter of the Earl. I hear the front door close and the first sob escapes me. I try to be brave, hold them back, but they will not be stopped.

Suddenly he is standing at the door. Through swimming eyes I watch him come to me. He sits beside me, pulls the vibrator out; it makes a sucking sound. He switches it off and bending his head licks a tear from my cheek.

'Damn you, Blake,' I whisper.

He buries his face in my hair. 'I'm sorry,' he says.

I stare at the ceiling. I am sadder than I have ever been. The doctor, the solicitor, Fleur, Madam Yula, The Fat Duck. 'Are you re-creating everything so you can destroy it, Blake?'

'No.'

'What do you want?'

'I thought I knew, but I don't anymore,' he confesses honestly.

'What did you want?'

'Revenge. I wanted to punish you. I had all kinds of humiliations planned for you, but I can't hurt you without hurting myself. Maybe you are what my father said you are. My greatest enemy.'

Automatically, my hands come up to wrap protectively around him. I know he is hurting too. I just don't know how to make it better. I want to tell him about Victoria, but what good would that do? She would make a new and supremely dangerous enemy. 'I'm not your enemy, Blake. I never meant to hurt you.'

He laughs. Again it is bitter. 'So what are you? A friend?'

I sigh. Such sadness is in that sound. Does he hear it? Possibly not. In his mind I am a gold digger. Took the money and ran. Now I represent dirty sex. There is a chasm between us. It seems impossible to bridge. From her ivory tower Victoria smiles triumphantly and tells me I am not embedded in his life plan. I will never be.

'Where do we go from here?'

He doesn't respond. Instead he gathers me in his arms and hides his face in the crook of my neck. Slowly he starts to suck. Automatically, my head twists away. Not in rejection, but in invitation. The dedication of his soft lips on my skin is delicious. His tongue burns a trail to my nipple. He takes it into his mouth and my humiliation, my hurt dissipates to nothing. Everything that happens between a man and a woman is a sacred journey, my mother once said.

She said that when my father left her.

A sound escapes my mouth. Silently, solemnly, he goes to the other breast. His teeth catch the nub and pull slightly. I writhe under the expert manipulation. He raises his head and looks at me as his palm skims the hardened tip. I am aching for him. Suddenly he is on his elbows and with consummate ease he pushes the entire length of his tongue into my aching folds. I grip the silky hair as his heated tongue thrusts in and out of me in sure practiced stokes. And then he begins to suck...

Ah, the pleasure, the pleasure!

He pinches my swollen clit in his fingers suddenly, and an intense pleasure like an electric current stabs me. I scream and come in a mindless explosion. Waves crash on the rocks below, but I fly high. When I come back to the bed and the room, Blake is still licking the wet walls of my sex. There will never be another after him, I think lazily, drowsily, sadly. He has done what he set out to do. Ruined me for all other men.

I am so drained and exhausted I close my eyes and fall asleep with the sensation of his silky head on my thighs.

Twelve

I wake up with the duvet pulled over my naked body, but alone. I turn my head and gaze at the vast expanse of bed that is spread out on one side of me and the unused pillows and sigh. Pushing my legs free of the duvet I dangle them out of the bed and savor the cool air. Then I slip out of bed. I can hear the fain sounds of Francesca, Blake's personal shopper, rummaging around in the kitchen. She is always as silent as a mouse. I pull on some clothes, brush my teeth, and go to the kitchen. She is updating her list on her iPad.

'Ciao,' she greets brightly. She is from Naples. 'I remember, you like jam and I bring you two extra bottles.' She holds them up in her expressive hands. 'You like?'

I go forward and take them in my hands. 'I like. Very much. Grazia, Francesca.'

She dimples prettily.

Tom drives Billie, Sorab, and me to The Royal China in Bayswater. We find a table and order our dim sums.

I take the bottles of jam out of my rucksack and stuff them into the back of Sorab's pram and Billie grins. 'The perks of pimping you out,' she says. 'By the way, Jack called me looking for you. Your mobile must have been switched off.'

'Oh! What did you tell him?'

'The truth, of course. You were with Blake.'

'What did he say?'

'He went dead silent for a while, and then he asked me if I thought you were safe. I said I didn't know, but that you thought you would be. Then he hung up.'

I bite my bottom lip.

'You should call him. He worries about you.'

'I will. This afternoon.'

'So how's it going at casa Blake?'

I expel my breath in a rush. 'I don't know, Billie. I might as well be a blow-up doll for all the use I am to him. It's really just sex. He's so remote, so angry, and so hurt. I don't believe I'll ever be able to reach him. He wants revenge, but he doesn't have the stomach for it.'

'What kind of revenge?' An edge has crept into Billie's voice.

'Sexual humiliation. Last night he used a…vibrator on me.' I flush bright red. The words were almost impossible for me to get out.

Billie laughs. 'You are so weird. That's not sexual

humiliation. Everybody uses them. If anyone offers to use one on me I'm going to lie back, open my legs as wide as they will go and ask them to knock themselves out.'

'You don't understand, Billie. He did it because he understands that I'm sexually repressed.'

'Oh for heaven's sake. You cried, didn't you?'

I nod and play with a chopstick. 'What would you do if you were me, Billie?'

'First off, I'm not you. I don't think I could ever be in such a fucked up situation.'

'But if you were,' I insist.

'Then I would drink at least half a bottle of vodka and challenge him to do his worst. Press all his buttons and push him mercilessly until he loses his tightly reined sense of control. And then it would all be over and done with. Mind you, I wouldn't if I thought he was capable of truly hurting me. But you're a thousand percent sure Blake is not, right?'

'A thousand percent. He is cold, not cruel.'

I pay the bill with the new Platinum credit card that I have not applied for, but arrived for me this morning. Billie raises an impressed eyebrow but says nothing.

Afterwards we spend a pleasant afternoon in Whiteley's Shopping Centre. There is nothing I want, but I treat Billie to a really cool pair of cowboy boots, which she adored, and we buy some divinely soft bedding for Sorab. Stuff I could never afford before.

Everything goes on the new card. It has a ninety

thousand pounds credit limit on it.

After Tom drops Billie and Sorab off I phone Jack.

'Are you all right?' is the first thing that Jack utters.

'He's not capable of hurting me, Jack,' I reply.

'It's not him I'm worried about.'

'Victoria won't do anything to me.'

'Lana, she paid you two hundred thousand pounds to get lost. You took her money and now you're back with her guy and you don't think she's going to retaliate?'

Oh God! Put like that it did seem I was being stupid in the extreme. 'I didn't go looking for him, Jack. He found me. Besides it's only for 42 days.'

'42 days?'

'He just wants me to finish my contract. There's 42 days left of it. Well, forty-one now.'

'Lana, I'm a man and I'm telling you no man wants a woman for just 42 days. It's not going to end in 42 days. I can give that to you in blood right now. You're going to be his mistress until the day comes when he is finally bored with your body. Is that what you want for yourself?'

That feels like a low blow and yet it is the truth. 'I don't know what I want anymore, Jack. All I know is at the moment I am with Blake for forty-one days. I'm playing it by ear.'

Jack sighs heavily. 'All right, Lana, but promise me you will take care of yourself, though. The first smallest sign that something is not right you will call me.'

'I promise. Jack?'

'Yeah?'

'Please don't worry about me. I'm a big girl now. I can take care of myself.'

'Just be careful, OK,' he says gruffly, and then he is gone. I lean back, but I do not think of Jack and his warning. Something else is bothering me.

As soon as I get into the apartment I go to my computer. Into the browser I type in the word cunt.

And I am shocked to learn that the word cunt is the most offensive word in the English language with the highest power to shock, but that it only became obscene around the time of Shakespeare. Before that it was actually the root word for the words queen and cuneiform, the most ancient form of writing. The word itself derives from kunta meaning female genitalia in Sumerian.

So: when a man calls a woman a cunt he is actually calling her the queen who invented writing and numerals —one of the finest compliments a woman can be given. The Irish apparently even use it as an endearment!

I also learn that cunt is the only word in the English language that describes the whole of the female genitalia. Vagina refers only to the inner entrance and vulva to the clitoris, outer labia majora and minora. To talk about a woman's entire incredible sexual orchestra in all its stupendous glory one needs the word cunt!

At that moment I claim the dreaded word for myself.

When Blake called me a cunt I had only pretended to

be offended. The real truth is that years of avoiding the word, and despising others for allowing something so foul and disgusting to sit on their tongues, fled and all I felt was its raw sexual pull. *Yes, I am a cunt and I want your rigid hot dick deep inside my cunt.* I realize that no matter what Blake said his actions were teaching me that my body is my temple. That between my legs is an altar called cunt where he comes to worship.

And now I have a plan. A plan that involves my cunt.

Thirteen

Blake sends a text to say that he will be around at 8:00 pm.

By seven thirty I am showered and standing in my new black stockings and garters. Carefully, I slip into the black dress that Fleur sent for me to wear to the opera and fasten the row of black pearl buttons. I look at myself in the mirror and marvel at the intricate beauty of the dress. It must have cost a small fortune.

The chest and the entire back is made of black patterned lace and lightly sprinkled with rhinestones, but the lace is so delicate it appears like a tattoo on my skin. I adjust the material into place around my body and hips, and then turn back to see the effect of the plunging back. It looks really cool and perhaps even sexy. I fluff out my hair and sit down to do my make-up. When I am done I slip into black stilettos and walk into the living room, the dress swirling gently around my shoes.

I pour myself a triple vodka and swallow it neat in four gulps. Wow! That makes my veins sing. I pour another double, top it up with orange and walk onto the balcony. I am actually very nervous. Make that very, very nervous. Tonight I will see him without his mask. I will provoke him into holding nothing back from me. I look at the time. 7:59 pm. I turn to find him standing at the door. He is watching me silently. Trying to figure out the scene he has come upon.

I turn fully. 'Hello.'

'Are we going out or are you dressed like that just for me?'

'We're not going out.'

An eyebrow rises. A mocking smile. He comes towards me. 'We're not?'

I shake my head slowly. 'I need a favor from you.'

'Are you allowed to ask favors?'

'You'll like this one.'

'You've got my attention.'

'I want you to hurt me.'

He becomes very still. For a moment neither of us says anything. We simply look at each other. And then he says, 'No.'

'Why not? I thought you wanted revenge.'

'I've tried rough sex and I didn't like it.'

I am shocked by the intense flash of burning jealousy that rips through me. He has already done this with someone else. There is no new territory that I may claim for my own. 'Maybe I do.'

His eyes narrow. They become like stones. Cold. Unreachable. They remind me of his father's eyes. I shiver involuntarily. Feel afraid. What if I am wrong? What if he is capable of really hurting me? 'What do you know about rough sex?'

'Show me what there is to know.'

'Is that what you really want?' His voice is soft, dangerously soft.

'Yes.'

His hands come up to my face. I cannot help it. I flinch and he smiles. A cold, knowing smile. Gently he brushes my cheeks with his hands. 'You're a baby. You don't know what you want,' he says, and he is about to turn away when I swing my arm with all my might and let my palm crash into the side of his face. I hit him so hard his head jerks away, and my hand is stinging painfully. The alcohol has made me strangely light-headed. I even feel removed from my own actions. I stare with dull fascination at his cheek, at the white imprint of my fingers. My eyes travel to meet his. They are stormy and furious.

'Feeling better?' he asks.

As an answer I swing my hand clumsily out again, but he is prepared this time and he catches my hand easily. I rush towards him and bite his neck. Hard. His growl is annoyed.

'You inherited all this money so everybody treats you like some kind of god, but you're just a little coward hiding behind a façade of superiority; a spoilt rich kid who has to do anything and everything Daddy tells him to do.'

He begins to laugh, really laugh, and suddenly I realize I have never seen him happy. Never seen his head thrown back and his throat open and vulnerable.

'I wonder what you would be without great-granddaddy's money?' I taunt.

'I'd still want to fuck you senseless.'

'Fuck you,' I shriek and as if possessed by some crazed demon I begin to kick at his legs and punch his hard body with my free hand. Like a sack of potatoes I am lifted up by sheer male strength and thrown over his shoulder. For a moment the shock of being turned upside down stills me and then I continue to pummel his back as he takes me into our bedroom. 'You don't trust anyone, you don't love anyone, you're just an emotional bonsai,' I scream.

He hurls me on the bed. I fall on my side, winded but unhurt. My head is still, but fuck me, the room is spinning around like a merry-go-round. Still, the important thing is I have lost all fear and apprehension. My only goal is to goad him into losing that tight control that dictates his every move. I look at him, my eyes taunting him. 'Scared of a cunt, Barrington?'

His head jerks slightly with surprise. 'You really want rough sex?' he asks.

I nod.

His mouth twists. He unbuttons his shirt, yanks the ends out of his trousers. Opens his fly, flings his underpants behind him and takes a step to the edge of the bed.

'Here it is, my love,' he grates.

In one smooth moment he hauls me up, catches the hem of my long dress and flicks it over my head. He stands looking at me, upper body and head covered, but lower body obscenely sprawled with garters, stockings and inelegantly splayed legs. Then, before I have even recovered my balance, he grabs my hips, his fingers digging painfully into my flesh, and brings me to my hands and knees. He grips my ass and very roughly spreads apart the cheeks, kneading them as if they are two pieces of dough, and drives his dick into my wetness, so savagely that I actually cry out with the shock of it. That stops him cold as if he too is shaken by the ferocity and violence of his own thrust.

'Don't stop,' I hear myself say, in a voice I do not recognize.

And he slams again into me. This time he does not stop even when I cry out. My entire body becomes a rag doll shuddering and rocking to the deep thrusts. I want to scream, but I dare not for fear he will stop. His stomach continues to pound my spread ass. His hands travel up my sweat-slicked body, digging, grasping in an effort to push as deep into me as he can. He grinds my rear so hard into his groin that I feel him to the very ends of me.

Every thrust is torture, but in the hurt there is a strange and exquisite pleasure. After he comes, he bends forward, kisses my shoulder blades and slowly eases out of me.

My slit is so sore it stings, burns and throbs painfully as he withdraws. It is over, I think. Then I feel his mouth lightly licking the reddened, raw skin around my cunt. He slips his velvet tongue gently inside, but even that hurts like hell. I moan and he takes his tongue away, starts lightly sucking my clit. I forget how sore I am and come in a moment, white with shockingly intense pleasure. As if my nerves have been made more alive by the pain, the pleasure is far more powerful than anything I have experienced before.

I fall forward on my face. My body is aching everywhere and so tender, I don't think I will be able to sleep on my back. My last thought as I drift into blackness is that I haven't had dinner yet and he never lost control. Despite all my efforts not once did his cold exterior crack to reveal the real man inside. Now I know whatever he guards so carefully inside must surely be truly precious or ugly beyond words.

Fourteen

I wake up, my mouth sour, aching, and stiff—getting out of bed is a slow belly crawl. I can barely walk to the bathroom. A disheveled mess greets me in the mirror. I stare with fascination at my reflection. Very slowly and with great difficulty I unhook the row of black pearl buttons at the back of the dress and shrug out of it. I go to the end of the room where two mirrors meet and gasp in shock at the dramatic sight that greets me.

My back, hips, buttocks, and thighs are blue black. It looks like I have been run over by a truck.

I gingerly lower myself down on the toilet seat. The urine flow burns and the entire area is so sore I can hardly clean myself. Drinking without having consumed food has also left me with a throbbing headache. I step into the shower. Good move, Lana. It relaxes my muscles and makes me feel a little more normal.

Afterwards I dose myself with two 500mg paracetamols. In fifteen minutes Mr. Nair and I are sitting at the kitchen counter having coffee. I feel pretty normal.

After coffee I call Tom and tell him that today I am bringing Sorab to stay with me. I go downstairs at 9:30 am and Tom puts down the newspaper he is reading.

'Good morning.'

'Good morning, Tom.'

He opens the car door, but getting in draws a wince from me.'

'Are you all right?' Tom enquires with a look of concern.

'Just stomach cramps,' I say.

He nods and goes around to the driver's seat.

Billie is drying dishes. She throws a dishtowel over one shoulder and turns to me. 'You look a bit constipated,' she says by way of greeting.

'I tried your advice. Drank half a bottle of vodka and pushed his buttons last night.'

'Oh yeah?'

'He didn't want to play ball.'

'So why are you all scrunched up with pain?'

'I mean, I got the rough sex, but nothing else,' I say. 'He never said a word he should not have or retaliated in any way that would fall outside of rough sex.' I lower myself slowly onto one of the dining chairs while Billie looks on with an expression I cannot quite fathom.

I stay with Billie the whole afternoon making plans for our new business.

Blake texts to tell me he will be late so I leave after the rush hour traffic at six. I have dinner on my own. A simple meal of grilled cheese on toast with a slice of smoked salmon on top. It is wonderful to have Sorab with me. The flat doesn't seem so foreign and lonely. Afterwards we have a grand old time in the bathroom, him shrieking happily and splashing lustily and me laughing. It is at this moment that Blake appears at the door.

'Hi,' I say. I am actually very nervous. In my mind I still think Sorab looks a lot like Blake.

'Who do we have here?' he says, and comes into the room. I look at him in surprise. He stands over us looking at Sorab for a long time. Sorab is waving his hands at the new face excitedly, but my heart is in my mouth. What the hell is he looking at? Surely, there is no way he can tell it is his son? When he turns to look at me his eyes are neutral. We look at each other.

'Does he cry a lot?' he asks finally.

'No. Most night he will sleep right through,' I say quickly, my breathing, returning to normal.

'Good,' he says, and turning around goes out. I throw the sponge into the water. Shit. For a moment there I was really worried. I mean really. I take Sorab out of the water and as I dress and powder him I can hear Blake in the dining room. He is talking to someone on the phone.

He works steadily on and by the time he comes into the bedroom I am almost asleep.

I feel the mattress next to me depress with his weight and I open my eyes sleepily. He is sitting in the dark. He bends his head and kisses me. I am so startled I come awake. The kiss is gentle and soft. I open my mouth and the kiss deepens. Raw hunger starts eating my brain. I am aching and sore and yet I am still gagging for him. I feel his fingers slide down my body and tug at the rim of my knickers. His fingers press flat against my crotch.

'You are so wet,' he whispers and inserts a finger into me.

It burns all the way in, and I tense involuntarily.

Immediately he stills. 'What's the matter?'

'Nothing,' I mumble and light bathes us. I blink and squint. Blake's hands are lifting my gown. My knickers are being taken off and I am being turned over. 'Jesus Lana,' he gasps. Gentle hands turn me back to face him.

'I did that?' His face is shocked, pale, draped in regret. I would never have believed that he could look so shaken. This is a new Blake. One I cannot reconcile with the man I know. The change in his face and eyes is so great, it is like night and day. Could a few bruises really have such a grand effect on a man like him? I did not like the answer. There was more to this change. What, I did not know yet.

'I bruise easily,' I explain warily. 'It's not permanent.'

He doesn't answer. 'I'm sorry... I'm so very sorry. I can't believe I've done that to you.'

I shrug, still very suspicious of his niceness. 'It's not as bad as it looks. Hey, I pushed you to it, remember?'

He looks at me with a creased brow. 'Why did you?'

I look down. 'You know that song 'Wrecking Ball' by Miley Cryus. That's me. I wanted to break down your walls. You were so cold and distant with me all the time. I guess I used my body as the wrecking ball…'

'There are many things you don't understand, but you must believe me when I tell you, you are my sustenance, my oxygen. I need you desperately. In fact, right now, what I feel for you is the only part of me that feels human.'

I look at him in shock. 'What do you feel for—'

He lays his fingers flat against my mouth. 'Shhh. Please trust me that I have your best interest at heart, always…and it is not in your best interest to know any more than you do now.'

I am unhappy with his mysterious reply, but I nod my agreement. What choice do I have?

'Now I need you to make me a promise.'

'What sort of promise?'

'That you will not leave me before your 42 days are up. No matter what you hear or see, no matter who asks you to, you will not leave me.'

'Why?'

'Because I am asking you not to. Will you do this one thing for me?'

I shrug. 'OK.'

'No, say the words. It is very important that you

understand the importance of the promise that I am asking for.'

'I promise not to leave you until the 42 days are up.'

'Do not forget this promise you have made to me.'

'I won't, but what happens when the 42 days are up?'

He smiles. It is a sad smile. 'That will be your decision.'

'My decision? What do you mean?'

'No more talking tonight. Move over to your side of the bed.'

My eyes widen. 'Are you staying the night?'

'Mmnnn.'

Instead of scooting over I gently roll over and end up on my side, propped on my elbow. 'Do you want me to blow you?'

He shakes his head.

'Are you holding out for my ass?' I tease cheekily, daringly.

'I will have your ass, soon. I want to own every part of you. But not today. Today I just want you to curl up against me and sleep.'

And that is what we do. We go to sleep entwined, like two wise snakes.

Fifteen

By the time I wake up Blake is gone. I bring Sorab into the bed and lie watching him drink his milk while my brain incessantly replays Blake's intriguing and confusing words from the night before.

You must believe me when I tell you, you are my sustenance, my oxygen. In fact, right now, what I feel for you is the only part of me that feels human.

Other than my failed attempt at being a wrecking ball, nothing I can see has changed between us, and yet the coldly furious stranger who could barely stand for me to touch him is suddenly professing an emotion so deep that it makes my toes curl. And what was the insistence that I promise never to leave him until the 42 days are up all about? What were the things that I do not understand that he referred to and he obviously did not want to tell me about? I remember again his intense eyes. He seemed to be begging for something from me, and yet what was he begging for? Another thirty-eight days with me? Why? Nothing makes sense.

Jack's words come back.

No man wants a woman for just 42 days.

When Blake said it would be my choice, did he mean the choice to be his mistress? And what of Victoria, his patient paragon of spotless virtue? I have dealt with her and I know without any doubt that she will not allow such a scenario.

I kiss Sorab's head. 'What's Daddy up to, Sorab?' I ask, but he only sleepily sucks at his milk bottle.

The day passes lazily without incident. My movements are slow and languorous. The pain is beginning to subside. When I use the toilet there is no burn. I am excited by the idea of Blake inside my body again. I recognize that I am in a state of constant arousal.

Laura calls to say that Blake will be home for dinner, but not to prepare any food. She is ordering in for us. Chinese. 'Anything you particularly want?'

'Crispy Peking duck,' I say.

I hear the smile in her voice. 'Yes, that's a particular favorite of mine too, Miss Bloom.'

It is a fine day with only a little wind and at four in the evening I pack a book and take Sorab out in his brand new stroller into the park for some fresh air. The seat where I had been joined by the exuberant puppy is empty so I head for it. The sun is deliciously mild, but I do not put the hood of the pram down. Next summer he will be ready to play in the sun.

I eye him proudly and he blows bubbles and shakes his rattle violently. I am so incredibly in love with him. I look around. There is hardly anyone about and after a little while, I take my book out and begin to read. No more than ten minutes could have passed with Sorab contentedly playing with the little toys hung up on the hood of his pram when a woman comes up to us.

'Oh, but he is a daahling,' she croons.

I look up from my paperback smiling. 'Thank you.'

'What's his name?'

'Sorab.'

She swings her head suddenly towards me and I am stunned by the flash of alarm in her eyes. 'Why did you name your son so?'

I remember myself. 'He's not my son. I am babysitting for my friend.'

'Oh,' she says and straightens so I get to see her properly. She has medium brown hair, pink cheeks, and blue eyes, and is wearing an understated, but obviously very expensive coat. Her accent is very upper class, but there is something shrill about her eyes. It makes me itch to stand up and put myself between her and my son. I stand up and we are facing each other.

'Why did she give him such a name?'

'It is after the legend of Rustam and Sorab.'

'Do you know the story of Rustam and Sorab?'

'No,' I lie, immediately.

'It is the legend of a very great warrior who accidentally kills his own son in the battlefield, because when the boy was born his mother lied. She told the father he had no son, that she had borne a girl.'

I stare at the woman trying to control my horror, but by the expression on her face I am not succeeding. The irony had not hit me before. What have I unthinkingly done? Who is this woman? What is she to Blake, my son, and me?

'Who are you?'

'Who I am is not important. Do not be tempted to stay longer than your allotted time. You and your son are in grave danger. It may even already be too late. Don't trust *anyone*.'

'What are you talking about?'

'Beware of Cronus,' she says, her voice as dry as dust, and begins walking away.

'Hey, come back,' I call out, but she increases her speed, and quickly disappears from my sight. I sit back down because my knees will no longer support me. I know that woman. An evening breeze rushes past me. I force myself up and push the pram as quickly as I can back to the apartment. Inside, I rush to the computer and Google images for the fourth Earl of Hardwicke and his family. Up pops a picture of the woman.

I sit back. The memory of her perfume drifts past me. The rest is a blur of real fear. Of course, I recognize her. The resemblance is small, but noteworthy. She is

Victoria's mother, but there is something pitiful about her. She has lost something precious. True, her shrill eyes betrayed extreme fury, but beneath the rage, she was essentially telling me that she has had to suffer, and intolerably. But unlike her daughter she was not threatening me, but warning me so I could avoid a similar suffering in my own future. *Beware of Cronus.* Turn back now, Lana. Before it is too late.

My phone rings. It is Blake.

'Hi,' I mumble.

'You sound strange. Is everything all right?'

'Yes, I'm fine,' I say.

'I'm coming home early. Wait for me.'

'I'm here,' I say.

By the time Blake gets home I have stopped restlessly pacing the floor and stilled the tremor in my hands, but not the terrible fear in my heart. I am standing in the middle of the living room lost to some unknown dread, when Blake appears at the doorway. I turn towards him and suddenly I am filled with a new fear. Can I even trust him? I feel confused and frightened of what I do not know.

In a few strides he has covered the ground between us. 'What is it?'

I shake my head. 'Why are you back so early?'

'We are going to Venice.'

'Venice?' I repeat stupidly.

'Would you like that?'

'I can't. I have Sorab.'

'He will come with us. Laura has arranged five nannies for you to interview tonight. They come with the highest recommendation from the best nanny agencies in London. The nanny can help you here too until such time as you no longer need her.'

Why did no one warn me about this? My hands rise to my temples. 'A nanny?' The word is foreign on my tongue. The idea intimidating. Another woman taking care of Sorab.

'The first lady will arrive at seven and one every half hour after that until you find one that you think is suitable. I thought we could have an early dinner. Laura has ordered us Chinese for six o'clock, I believe.'

I nod distractedly and notice the relief that washes over his face and tense shoulders, but I cannot imagine why he is relieved.

'Can I fix you a drink?' he asks, and moves to the bar. I stare at his turned back. Suddenly I have the distinct impression, he is worried about something. Something important. Something about me. But he doesn't want to talk about it. Not yet. It's part of those secret things I do not understand.

'A large brandy,' I reply.

He pushes a goblet into my hand, kisses me softly on the forehead. 'I'll join you after a shower. Just relax. Be back soon.'

'Why are we going to Venice?'

'You are going to the opera to experience Venetian

music in its original setting. Pack your black dress,' he says, his eyes smoldering.

He has planned a Venetian adventure for me. I drop my eyes to the floor. *I dare not look in his eyes, not yet.* I plan to tell him about Victoria's mother. Not today, though. Not until I figure out who Cronus is. And who I can trust. Who is friend and who is foe?

The nannies arrive punctually. When the third woman comes through the door I know she is the one. She has a pleasant face and laughing, soft eyes. Her name is Geraldine Dooley. She is from Ireland. I put the baby in her arms.

'All right, lad, what's the story?'

Sorab babbles back at her.

'T'be sure,' she agrees solemnly.

The last two candidates I am able to cancel by calling their mobiles, but the next candidate is already waiting for me in the living room. I go out to meet her.

'I'm so sorry to have wasted your time. I have just found the nanny that is perfect for my son.'

She smiles and pulls on spotlessly white cotton gloves. 'You haven't, my dear. I have been paid a considerable amount for attending this interview on such short notice.'

A thought occurs to me. 'What time were you contacted?'

'I couldn't say for sure. But perhaps 4:30 pm.'

'Oh.' That was just after Victoria's mother

approached me in the park. Can it be a coincidence that I am suddenly being whisked off to Venice? Her words, 'trust no one,' still reverberate in my head. Perhaps it is naïve of me, but I am unafraid. I believed him when he asked me to trust him to do what is in my best interest. And I still do.

With his hands spanning my waist just above the bruises and his eyes never leaving mine, Blake gently lowers me onto his throbbing hardness. The muscles in his jaw twitch and betray his lack of detachment. I know he is worried about hurting me, but I am so slick and wet and ready that the first inch slips in easily, filling and opening me beautifully. It feels so good I drive myself down and suddenly he has pierced me too deeply, stretched the swollen hole too much. I cry out involuntarily and I feel his hands bodily lift me off the shaft I am impaled on.

'Jesus, Lana. Take it easy,' he bites out.

But now that the first flash of pain is gone I am afire with need. I want to forget about Cronus and Victoria and all the confusing things I have not yet figured out and I know no better way. I place my hands on either side of him and slowly push my trembling, clinging sex down until the bruises on my rear touch his thighs. I stop and move upwards. This exquisite pain-pleasure is what I have been craving all day. This time I go down that bit faster. My soaked sex hovers an instant at the tip of his shaft and then comes down too hard. I cry out.

He tries to hold me up.

I shake my head and say, 'No, this is fine. I can take it.'

He tightens his grip around my waist.

'No. No more pain for you,' he says firmly, and gently rolls me onto my back. He covers my entire body with daddy-long-legs kisses until I feel as if I am floating. And when I do come, I feel as if I am a pond on a day when the sunlight is so white it is impossible to look at it. And someone goes and throws a stone into the pond of my very core, the shimmering ripples spreading out and out and out.

Sixteen

I stand on the prow of the black boat that traverses the Grand Canal to catch the full opulence and majesty of the white domes of the church in the bright sunlight. Such decoration, such grandeur. A funereal gondola passes us. I shiver and touch the blue ribbon that Blake has put in my hair. Here even decay and death are beautiful. Rotting houses stand next to glorious palaces.

Blake extends a strong arm down to me at the Piazza San Marco stop. He is dressed in a black denim shirt rolled up at the sleeves, blue jeans and lumberjack boots, and is head and shoulders taller than most of the locals. Devilishly sexy dark sunglasses do not allow me to see his eyes. I look up at him with that same sense of awe that he is with me. He helps me off the boat and keeps my hand as we walk up to the piazza.

I immediately fall in love with the regiments of arches

that surround the impossibly splendid square. The great flocks of pigeons that roost in the stupendous roofs fly down to interact amiably with the tourists clutching guidebooks and cameras. They flutter around us and make me smile.

We stop for coffee. The waiter brings biscotti with our coffee. Blake pushes his sunglasses over his head, stretches his long legs out in front of him, and closing his eyes turns his face up to the sun. I dip a biscotti into my cappuccino. The dunked biscotti reminds me of the tide marks on the stained, crumbling walls.

'The lagoon is eating the city alive,' I say.

Blake looks at me. 'It submits with pleasure to the tide. It's a willing consummation. The way I have been crumbling into you from the first night I laid eyes on you.'

For a moment we are both lost in each other's gaze. And then I simply can't leave it; I whisper, 'But what happens after the 42 days are up?'

A strange emotion crosses his eyes. Pain? Sorrow? 'I don't ever want to lie to you. The truth is I don't know. There are powerful forces at play, predictable only in their ruthless ability to accumulate and re-create the world in their image. And I am part of that image.'

I frown. These riddles. What does he mean? 'What forces?'

'Forces that are unaccountable, unprincipled, and extremely dangerous. The less you know the safer you will be. I may never tell you about them. I take them on willingly for you, but I might lose. The only way you can help me is to keep your promise. No matter what you hear, see or whatever anyone tells you, do not forget your promise.' Then his mouth stretches into a brilliant smile. And that smile takes my breath away. 'Will you trust me that even if I lose, I will ensure that you will be taken care of for life?'

Money! I don't want his money. I want to know what he knows. I want to have him, forever.

I let my gaze drop and he reaches forward and covers my hand with his. His hand radiates warmth. I turn my palm upwards and entwine my fingers with his. I realize that this is a moment of great import. I look up. I am looking into the eyes of a man who almost appears to be drowning and I am the straw that he has found to clutch onto. For the first time I realize that beneath the cold, aloof exterior there is so much, so much more depth. I smile suddenly.

'All right,' I say. 'Let's live as if all we have left are thirty-seven days. Let's not waste a second.'

'That's my girl,' he says, and standing up tugs my hand. 'Come on,' he urges. 'To know Venice one must wander its narrow bridges and bewildering alleys on foot.'

We leave the winding alleys to stop for lunch in an old ostaira that apparently has been around since the nineteenth century. Blake and I both order the pasta in squid ink to start, followed by baked swordfish and polenta, which the waiter tells us are the house specialty.

Pasta in squid ink is something I have never tried before, and I enjoy it very much, but the portions are very large and I leave nearly half of my main course behind.

Blake frowns. 'Your appetite was better before. You have lost so much weight. Why?'

I shrug. 'I'm sorry. The food is delicious, but I really can't have any more.

'He looks at me, his fork neatly laid at the four o'clock position on his plate, waiting for an explanation.

I glance down at my hands. They are clenched tight. 'For weeks after what happened to Mum, I couldn't eat at all. Every time I thought about food I saw that breakfast table again. It is almost as if my stomach has shrunk and I can only eat small amounts.'

'What breakfast table?'

I unclench my hands and flex my fingers. I haven't spoken to anyone, not even Billie, about that day when I opened the front door and even the walls were silently screaming for my mother. I look up.

'I had an appointment with the doctor that day. My mother wanted to come, but I said to her, "No, I'll be fine." God, I wish I had never said those words. If only I'd kept my mouth shut and let her come with me, she might be alive today.'

I shake my head with regret. 'I can still see her face. "Are you sure?" she asked. Even then I could have said, "All right, come. You can keep me company." But I didn't. Instead, I said, "Absolutely. Stay at home and have a rest. Hospitals are full of germs."

'When I came back, I opened the front door and called to her. She did not answer so I went into the kitchen, and I knew immediately that something was very wrong when I saw the kitchen table. It should have been ready for lunch, but it was full of leftovers from our breakfast. Sliced tomatoes, pita bread, olives, oil. And... flies.' I cover my mouth. 'Flies were buzzing around the congealed fried eggs.'

The startlingly clear image makes me feel nauseated again and I push the plate of food away from me and take a deep, steadying breath. I do not tell him that that day too my milk dried up. Not a drop was left for Sorab. A kindly woman, two doors away became his wet nurse until the day I left Iran.

I look up into his eyes and they are soft and pained. In his world of unlimited funds almost everything can be made better with a little application and cunning. This one cannot. Even he is helpless in the face of death.

'She was such an incredibly clean person. I knew something terrible had happened. My mother had gone out to the shop opposite to buy some sugar for her coffee and had been run over while crossing the road outside our house. For many weeks I would wake up having dreamt of flies in my food. Perhaps it was the shock of how quickly they had taken over my mother's kitchen, after her relentless efforts of keeping them away.'

My chest seizes up. A small sob escapes. Oh no, surely I'm not going to bawl again. I swallow while the tears run down my cheeks. I feel the waiter's eyes on me. Blake reaches for my hand.

'I'm sorry,' I apologize, squeezing his hand. 'I know, this too will pass, and all that, but I just can't seem to get over my loss.'

After lunch we return to the palazzo that belongs to Blake's family. Iced with a filigree of white stone and built on three floors it reminds me of a wedding cake. Inside, it is as beautiful as any palace with glittering mosaic, marble statues of human beings, golden statues of beasts, detailed frescos, decorated ceilings, priceless antiques, bell pulls made of rich gold and red braids, and liveried servants

Gerry is sitting on the balcony under an umbrella. Sorab squeals with delight at my appearance. The afternoon is spent on the balcony with Sorab. Pleasant. Rare. I won't ever forget it.

That evening I go to the top floor. A strange place. Smooth marble steps right in the middle of the huge space lead to an antique clawed bath with gold taps. I take my dressing gown off and step into the scented water. Here the servants are light-footed and like ghosts. Secretive and almost unseen. I rest my head against the warm marble.

High above my head looming out of the dark of the vaulted roof space is an iron chain from which a glass chandelier of unsurpassed beauty is suspended. Its many glass arms twist and turn into delicate cristallo cups that hold real candles. Blake told me that it was once made for the Church of Santa Maria della Pieta, but one of his more flamboyant ancestors acquired it for himself. He wanted to look up at the work of art as he bathed. At the hundreds of diamond fruits and crystal teardrops.

I gaze at them with awe. Each droplet, because of its position on the chandelier and its distance from each candle, has been blown a slightly different shape in order to transmit the same luminescence from every angle as they capture the flickering flames inside their prisms.

Blake appears at the door. He stands in the enormous shadows cast by the candles. Silent, full of some wild emotion that makes my cheeks burn.

'I've dreamed of seeing you in this bath under this chandelier,' he says huskily, and, coming forward into the light, takes the washcloth out of my hands and proceeds to wash my back.

I feel his mouth on the back of my neck; the evening stubble of his unshaved face rasps my skin. Goose pimples rise on my exposed skin. Instantly my head arches back exposing my entire throat to him. He kisses my neck softly, delicately. His large hands catch my breasts. Immediately, the desire for him grows in my being. I want him inside me, but he shakes his head lightly.

'No, no, I have other plans for you.' He stands up and brings the towel. I stand, soapsuds running down my body. Hoping he will change his mind. His eyes darken, but he wraps the towel around me carefully and turns me around in his arms.

'I love you,' I say.

He stills. Something indescribably beautiful comes into his eyes. 'I know,' he says gently. 'It is what keeps me going.' But he does not say I love you back. Instead he helps me into my dressing gown. 'Fabiola is waiting outside to do your hair.'

'Oh.'

Someone outside to do my hair. I look at him in wonder, at the precision of his plans. Is there anything he has not thought of? Fabiola enters with a rosewood box. In its compartmentalized interior she keeps all her accoutrements. She is young, keeps her dark eyes lowered for most of her time with me, and does not speak English, but she is nothing short of a hair genius. She twines blood-red rosebuds into my hair. It is the kind of hairdo that you see on Oscar night. I will be sorry to see it come down.

When she is gone I dress in the black gown. There is only one yellowing bruise that shows through the net on my lower back. I twist up the scarlet lipstick and apply it to my lips. I get into my tall shoes and in the mirror a woman looks back, highly colored, wild-eyed, and more than a little wanton, but at the same time, rather beautiful. I am still looking at my reflection when Blake comes into the room. My breath catches. He is dressed in a black tux. I have never seen him look so vital and handsome. His hair gleams. With that aristocratic nose…he looks like he has just stepped out from a painting.

He is carrying two packages in his hands. He comes and stands behind me. Inside the looking glass we make a stunning couple. I don't make any sudden movements; I don't want to spoil it for the woman in the parallel universe. Perhaps she will get her man. All day long, people have been staring at us. Now I know why. He opens the first package and takes out a necklace. It is stunningly simple. A band made of rubies with an oval black centerpiece.

'It's a black diamond,' he says.

'It is beautiful,' I breathe, raising my eyes to meet his.

'Something for you to remember Venice by.' He sets it around my neck. The red stones encircle my throat like ribbons of fire. He stands back and looks at me. There is a glint of possessive pride in his eyes. And I feel owned.

Then he opens the next box.

I tilt my head forward curiously. 'What are they?' I ask. I cannot make them out. On a bed of black material are some colorful gadgets made of plastic or silicon.

His answer is succinct. 'Spread your legs.'

My body's reaction is immediate. A wave of sexual arousal. Those things fit into my body. I obey. He bends and, lifting the long dress, inserts one of them into me, adjusts it so the cup-like end fits snugly around my clitoris, and pulls my knickers up over it. It feels strange and smooth inside me. From his trouser pocket he takes out a small device. It is no bigger than a remote control car key. He presses it and the thing inside me starts vibrating.

'Oooo,' I giggle. As he turns the dial the vibrations become more violent until I squeal, 'Hey.'

He turns it right down.

'Venetian music in its original setting *and* the latest vibrator,' I tease, but I am fascinated with the idea of putting total control of my sensations into his hands.

'It is the perfect touch,' he says softly. 'Music is passion. We are going to watch L'Incoranazione di Poppea. The coronation of Poppea is a Venetian opera of unbearable sensuousness, and the frissons you will experience on the outside will be reflected inside your body.'

Seventeen

The sun is bleeding into the lagoon as we go down the steps and climb into the gondola. It is a cool evening and his arm comes around me. I revel in his touch. I know Cronus is waiting for me in England, but this is my night, my adventure. He is not allowed here, in this sinking city.

The theater is very old and full of faded charm. There are no tourists present. The other patrons who have turned up are mostly elderly and dressed in fine clothes. They have a kind of grave dignity that reminds me of a time gone by. Everyone seems to know everyone else and one or two of them even nod gravely to Blake. It is almost as if it is a private showing. We take our place in one of the boxes.

'This theater affords better acoustics than some of the more glamorous ones,' Blake explains, before the curtain goes up, and the vibrator begins its almost constant throb. At first, I squirm awkwardly, judging it as an unwelcome distraction that is going to reduce my enjoyment of the experience of being at the opera, but then I begin to look for its rhythm.

It soars with the music.

The opera is sung in Italian, but I have Blake whisper in my ear each scene and even point out the significance of some arias. The coronation of Poppea charts the opulently atmospheric journey of Poppea, the mistress of the Roman emperor Nero, who in pursuit of her desire to be Empress of Rome forsook love for the power. As Blake warned, the story is erotic and decadent. Combined with the vibrator between my legs the experience is indescribable and has me not only incredibly aroused, but also emotionally drained, and perhaps confused too.

During the rapturous love duet when Nero holds Poppea in his arms while she caresses her jeweled crown, and the vibrator has been turned to full, I turn to look at Blake wondering why he has brought me to see an opera where the virtuous are punished or put to death and the greedy and unscrupulous rewarded. Is it an unsubtle hint to me? Am I the greedy woman of his world?

As if he has read my mind he says, 'Glorious music goes beyond human frailties.'

It is true I feel excited and light-headed. The experience has been profound. I need to go the toilet and see what I look like. It feels as if I have been altered this evening. I touch his wrist lightly. 'Going to the toilet. Meet me at the bottom of the stairs.'

He nods and stands. Between my legs I am throbbing. I don't know if he can see the desire in my eyes. I don't want to go to dinner. I just want to go home and have him inside me.

In the faded mirror I meet myself. My eyes are strange. I am changing right before my eyes. I touch the slightly protruding cup on my clitoris and think about taking it out, but in my heart that privilege belongs only to Blake. He put it in there and he is entitled to take it out when it suits him.

Coming down the curving marble stairs from the toilets, I witness him in conversation with one of the ushers. A raven-haired girl. His back is to me and he is speaking to her in Italian. I see her animated face and a strange unfamiliar fear clutches at my stomach. Immediately, I grasp the wrought iron and brass banister, unsteady suddenly, my heart knocking painfully against my ribs. Whatever he has said has made her laugh self-consciously, and, as I watch, her large, dark eyes kindle with fiery interest.

I lay my palm flat on my stomach almost in disbelief. I am jealous. I am unreasonably, insanely, uncontrollably jealous of a man whom I cannot even publicly lay claim on. But the thought of him with anyone else makes me feel sick to my stomach.

Will it always be so from now on?

The most innocent encounters ripe for worry and painful inner speculation while I play blind, deaf and dumb outwardly? Then he turns, his eyes searching, looking for me, and I step forward, a silent sigh escaping my lips, relieved to be back in the warm, wonderful light of his gaze. And everything is fine again; the fear slinks away, momentarily.

'I didn't know you spoke Italian?'

He grins. 'Nope, but I studied Latin in school, so it's not difficult to figure out how to ask for directions.'

With the dark water lapping at the steps of the Palazzo, I whisper, 'Blake can we go upstairs first... before we eat.'

He shakes his head with a smile. 'Not yet, Principessa.' He puts his hand into his pocket and the little machine buzzes into life. But now the suction cup is licking me almost like a tongue.

'Oh, Blake,' I gasp. 'I can't take much more of this.'

'Yes, you can,' he says.

I swallow hard. How can I think of food while my pussy is throbbing and a silicon tongue is licking my clit? The only thought on my mind is release. I am already very close to climax.

'What if I have an orgasm at the dinner table?'

'You won't. I'm switching it off while you eat. Nothing comes between you and food.'

I gape at him.

'Have I ever told you, Miss Bloom, you're a sight to behold,' he says cheekily, and pulls me up the steps.

He goes through the double doors of the salon and I

go upstairs to check on Sorab. Mercifully the vibrator stops as I am walking up the stairs. Sorab is fast asleep. Gerry's door is slightly ajar and light is coming through. I knock softly.

'Come in,' she says.

I enter. She is in bed reading. Her kind face is wreathed in a welcoming smile.

'How was he?'

'As good as gold.'

'I'll keep him tomorrow morning and you can take some time off. Do some sightseeing.'

'No need for that, Love. I was here twenty years ago. Broke my heart on a glass blower.'

And it occurs to me that it is impossible to tell the nuances of anyone's history by looking at them or knowing them for a few days. My mother used to say, 'You can eat salt with someone for five years and never know them.'

I find Blake in the cavernous, gorgeously painted red dining room. He is standing by the fireplace looking up at a massive portrait of a haughty man in fine clothes. He turns at my approach. The resemblance between him and the man in the portrait is striking. It is immediately apparent that he is an ancestor. It is there in the aristocratic arch of his cheek, the set of his jaw. The same way that I found Victoria in her mother. These families that do not mix their blood easily carry their genetic footprint clearly in their faces, their bearing.

The humming between my legs begins as I walk

towards him.

'Have your family always owned this house?'

He frowns. Discussions about his family always distance him. 'Yes, we are descended from the Black Venetians. We branched out into Germany before crossing the Atlantic.'

'It's very beautiful. Do you come here often?'

'I haven't been to this house for years,' he replies, and switches on the licking function.

I squirm.

'Shall we eat?'

Dinner is served by a dour, mostly silent man in a white jacket called Enzo. I find it almost impossible to eat. True to his word Blake has switched off the gadget, but by now I am so aroused I can hardly wait for the meal to be over. I taste nothing. When Blake pushes away his coffee cup I spring up.

'What's the rush? You'd only be exchanging the silicon tongue for mine.'

I make a strangled sound and turn pleadingly towards him. 'Please, can we go up *now*?'

'No, I want to see you completely laid to waste tonight,' he says, lifting the champagne bottle and filling our glasses. 'I am going to make you come harder than you have ever done before,' he promises as the licking and vibrating in my knickers increase in tempo.

I sit down and lift the glass to my lips. It is a beautiful, hand-blown work of art. The long slender stem rises into a decorative figure of the lion of St.

Mark's before it meets the delicate flute.

'Mmnnn.' He takes my wrist in his hands and runs his finger lightly along the inside, up to the crook of my elbow. The sensation is unbearably sensual. The desire to straddle him in that vast red room is undeniable.

'I have never met a woman with skin like yours,' he purrs. He looks into my eyes. 'Do you have any idea how desirable you look right now?'

I clench my thighs and shake my head.

We go up the curving staircase to our bedroom. Moonlight is flooding in through the tall windows. There are long rectangles of light on the floor.

He turns to me and gently takes off my dress. He throws it behind him and it lands on a squat green and gold brocade chair. He drops to his haunches, bends forward and kisses the tightly bound mound of my sex. The gesture is so unexpectedly charged with erotic possibilities that my body screams for him. He slides my knickers off.

'Spread your legs.' I obey instantly. He removes the gadget and I actually feel my body sag with relief. He lets his fingers graze the sticky opening. 'You are so, so wet,' he says.

I nod helplessly. My hands are frustrated fists, waiting for him.

'What do you want, Principessa?'

'You.'

He shakes his head gently. The eyes looking up at me are almost black. 'I need more details. The low-down of what you want.'

'I need you inside me,' I mutter.

Again his head moves negatively. 'Details, Lana. Details.'

And in this way he persuades me to describe in minute detail exactly what I want, to use words that would have at any other time made me blush furiously. That thick prick of yours, your dirty big, cock, deep into my cunt, suck it, fuck me hard...

He gags me. 'The walls are thin and may even have ears,' he whispers. It jars in my head, but only a little; I am too far gone to search for hidden implications.

His large hands grab my hips and impale me on his dick.

The pillar of solid meat is thrust far into my body. Instead of moving me up and down the hard length, he pulls me to and fro, making me ride him like a bull. I grind myself on him. My body is thrust far forward like one of those cyclists in the tour de France race, so that his mouth has easy access to my breasts.

He latches on and sucks hard and my sweaty thighs slip and slide against his muscular hips, the thick cock inside me acting as my brakes. It is too intense to last. In seconds I lose it. Screaming like a banshee, I come fast and hard. Thank God for the gag. I have lost it. Completely. Even my teeth, fingertips and toes are vibrating.

I rest my lips on his damp forehead. Sated. He is still hard as a rock inside me. My nipples are still pinched between his thumbs and forefingers. They throb painfully, exquisitely. Now it is his turn. And then it will be mine again. The day will come when all I will have are memories of what we have done together.

I am awakened in the early morning hours. Must be the unfamiliarity of my surroundings. It is two o'clock and it seems all of Venice is asleep. I get out of bed and walk barefoot across the highly polished dark wood floor, towards the windows overlooking the interlocking canals and cobblestone pathways. Shivering slightly I stand in the cool night listening to the sounds of the murky waters lapping against mossy, old stones. The sulfuric smell like that of slowly rotting eggs rises from the canals and slips into my consciousness. Not that that bothers me. For me being with Blake in this city with its crumbling glory and beautiful stonework is a dream.

And then a thought—clawed and dangerous. Who or what is Cronus?

I hear a rustling and, turning my head, see Blake, raised on his elbows and watching me. In the silvery moonlight he is Atlas or Mars or Apollo. A god. He gets out of bed, nude, and with the lithe grace of a beautiful animal, prowls over to me. He bends and kisses me. I luxuriate in the warmth emanating from the length of his body. But my thoughts make me kiss him a touch too desperately.

He lifts his head and looks at me. In the moonlight his eyes are dark wells of curiosity.

'What's the matter?' he asks, crouching beside me.

'Nothing,' I lie. 'I think I'm too excited to sleep.'

He sighs and persists, 'What's wrong, Lana?'

'What did you say to the usher at the theater?'

He sits back on his heels. 'What usher?'

'You know, when I went to the toilet.'

'Ah... I was asking if there was an ice cream bar nearby. Why?'

I look down, unable to meet his eyes, unable to help the sadness that creeps into my voice. 'I just wondered if you...if you found her attractive.'

'What?'

I look up at him.

He takes my cold fingers in his large warm hands. 'Shall I tell you a secret?'

I nod. That will be a first.

'From the first moment I saw you I wanted you. Not in the compartmentalized way I wanted the others, the length of leg, the jut of a butt, or the strain of material caused by a well-shaped chest. When I saw you I had to have all of you as mine. I would have paid any price that night to buy you.'

'Oh, Blake,' I sigh. I want him to say he loves me, even if it is just a little, but I won't push anymore, I might hear something I don't want to. It is always cleverer to quit while still ahead.

'Shall I show you just how much I want you?' he asks quietly.

I nod and he stands up. I stretch my arms out to him

as if I am a child, and he picks me up and carries me to the kingly bed. I sigh deeply with pleasure under him. For a time there is only the soft rustle of white linen and the occasional gasp. Then a fierce, rapid rhythm. Until a shudder like a silver explosion shivers through me, and I am back among glittering stars. Here I can hide from Cronus. I hold onto the exciting firmness of his buttocks as he finds his release and spills his seed inside my body.

Dreamily I snuggle deeper into his body and am soon as deeply asleep as everybody else in that stinking, sinking city.

Eighteen

After a trip to the glass blower's we return the way we came. By private plane: without queues, passport control or waiting for baggage. Blake does not get into the car with us. He has a business appointment that he must keep. He tries to convince me to let the nanny go back to the apartment with me, but I refuse. She is put into a taxi.

I hold Sorab in my lap and stare out of the window. I cannot help feeling a little depressed. While I was away I had temporarily put away the things that Victoria's mother had said, but now they have all come crowding back. Their whispers are loud in the quiet apartment. I feel very alone and frightened.

When Jack calls I immediately invite him to come around.

'You've just come back from holiday. You must have a thousand things to do. I won't disturb you. I'll come tomorrow,' he says.

'No, not at all. Do please come today, now if you can. I'd love to see you again.'

'Is everything all right, Lana?'

I laugh. 'Of course. I just want to see my son's godfather again. Is there anything wrong in that?'

He laughs. The sound is familiar. 'No, but you will tell me if there is, won't you?'

'Yes, yes, yes. Now how long will it take you to get here?'

'Half an hour.'

'See you then.' I terminate the call and feel relief.

'Mr. Jack Irish at reception for you, Miss Lana,' Mr. Nair calls thirty minutes later.

'Brilliant. Send him up,' I say, and opening the front door go out to wait by the lift. The lift opens and there is Jack. He doesn't look comfortable. I can see he is overawed by his surroundings.

'My, my, Jack,' I say, 'is that a new shirt? I don't think I've ever seen you in red.'

He flushes. 'Alison picked it out,' he mumbles, and steps out of the lift.

'Hey, it looks good. Really. Actually, very dashing.'

'And you're playing fast and loose with your compliments today.'

'I am,' I agree, and go into his arms. It is so familiar. So good. I love Jack. I truly do. He is like that first ray of sunshine after a particularly heavy downpour. A delicious uncomplicated invitation to go out and play. I step away. 'Come and see the place.'

I push open the door and turn around. 'Wow,' Jack says. 'This place must have cost something.'

'Yeah, wait till you see the view.' I pull him by the hand towards the balcony.

'Startling, isn't it?'

'Vistas like this must surely induce attacks of megalomania,' he says softly. We stand in silence for a minute, and then he turns to me. 'Where's the brat then?'

'Sleeping.'

'Again?'

I laugh. It is so easy with Jack. 'Want some real coffee?'

'What kind of question is that?'

'Come on then.'

I put on some music and we sit on the sofa with our cappuccinos.

'Just off the top of your head, what do you know about Cronus?'

'That's a strange question.'

I take a sip of the hot liquid. 'Just heard it the other day and realized I didn't know anything about it.'

'My Greek mythology is very shaky, but I believe he is the god who ate his own children. It is also another name for Saturn, or Father Time.'

'The god who ate his own children?'

'Yeah, it was to stop a prophecy that his own child

would overthrow him. Something like that, anyway.'

I nod unhappily. Don't like the sound of any of it. After Jack leaves I intend to do my own research.

'Are you happy, Lana?'

'No,' I say before I can stop myself.

His coffee cup freezes on its way to his lips.

I cover my mouth with the tips of my fingers. I can't tell him about Cronus so I start making it up. 'No, wait. That came out wrong. I'm not actively unhappy.' I clasp my hands under my chin. 'But you know how I feel about him. It's a kind of torture to be so in love with someone who doesn't love you back. I'm the dead wasp floating in his glass of champagne. I ruin his perfect life. His perfect plans.' And yet this too is true. Blake is not happy. There is something that is tearing his insides, but he won't tell me what it is.

Jack puts his coffee cup on the low table. 'You poor duck,' he says with such compassion, I am suddenly filled with morbid self-pity. I blink back the tears. Jack puts his hand out.

'Don't touch her.'

The violence in the words startles me. I swing my head around and find Blake standing at the door of the living room. We had not heard him enter. The thick carpets, the music.

His face is a thundercloud. I jump up guiltily, my face flaming. And then I realize I have done nothing wrong. We have done nothing wrong. My innocence makes my voice strong. 'We were just talking, Blake. Jack is my brother.'

Blake does not look at me. 'He's not your brother. He's in love with you.'

'Oh! For God's sake,' I burst out angrily, and turn to Jack in exasperation for support against such a distorted view of our relationship, and then I freeze.

Jack is looking at me with so much pain in his tortured, artist's eyes. Why, Blake is right. My Jack is in love with me. Deeply. Hopelessly. Perhaps for years. It seems impossible. It is me who has been so blind, so stupid. Both our mothers knew it.

'Jack?' I whisper. I want him to deny it so it can all be as it was before—uncomplicated, beautiful, but he presses his lips into a thin line and starts walking towards the door. Blankly, I follow his progress past Blake, their shoulders almost brushing but not quite. He is in the corridor when I find my legs and begin to run after him. Blake catches me by the arm.

'Let me pass,' I hiss.

He looks at me. Implacable, his eyes glittering. 'I don't share,' he rasps.

'Please... He needs me now'

'Your pity is the last thing he needs.'

'I wasn't offering pity. I was offering friendship.'

'He doesn't want your friendship either. He wants you in his arms, in his bed. Can you give him that, Lana?'

We stand there staring at each other, the air bristling. Then he releases my arm and backs away from me. I drop my head. As I stand there crushed by my loss, he puts his arms around me and draws me to his body. 'I'm sorry, baby.'

I lay my cheek against his hard chest. Dry-eyed. When the loss is that big tears don't come. I know from the time I lost my mother. Tears come when you release that person and I refuse to release Jack. He will fall in love with someone else. He will forget this love he has for me and then we will be brother and sister again. I feel Blake's lips on my hair.

And I begin to cry. Not for the loss of Jack because I will never lose Jack, but for the loss of Blake, because I know in my heart of hearts I can't keep him. Because of Cronus; because everything I really love is always being taken away from me. Blake doesn't understand why I am crying or clinging or why I am insatiable. I am drinking the last of the summer wine. That night I let myself get drunk as a skunk.

Nineteen

When I go to visit Billie she has a surprise for Sorab. A beautiful rocking horse from Mamas & Papas.

'OMG!' I exclaim. 'You shouldn't have. That must have cost a fortune,' I go to it and touch the soft brown material of the horse's mouth.

'Nah, I nicked it.'

I whirl around to face her. Trying to imagine how on earth she walked out of the store with such a big item in her arms. 'Why, Billie?'

She shrugs. 'It's not a big deal. These big corporations make allowances for pilferage. It's part of their operating costs.'

'When we have our business are we going to make allowances for pilferage too?'

'Hell, no.'

I raise my eyebrows and cross my arms over my chest.

'All right,' she says. 'But I'm not taking it back.'

I laugh. Billie is incorrigible. Sometimes I wish I was like her. Life is such an abundant adventure. She takes everything with both hands.

'Listen, Billie, I know why you did it, but you don't have to compete with Blake. You're Sorab's aunt. You'll always be there,' and the words stick in my throat, but I spit them out, 'Blake will not.'

'I'm sorry, Lana.'

'You don't have to apologize to me.'

'I'm sorry that you can't have Blake.'

'Yeah. It's a bummer.'

'I got a bottle of vodka,' she suggests brightly.

I smile. 'No, but I'll have a cup of tea, though.'

We are sitting at the kitchen table having our tea when the doorbell rings.

'Expecting someone?'

'Yeah, Jack said he might come around.'

'Oh!'

She goes to open the door. 'Hey, you.'

'Hey, yourself,' Jack says and comes in.

'Hello, Jack,' I greet softly.

'Hello, Lana.' He is surprised to see me. His eyes seem sad. So sad. I don't think I have ever seen him like this. Now that his secret has been unmasked he seems purposeless, empty and defeated. He looks like a man who has had all his dreams and hopes shattered, and he is simply standing there looking at the shards in disbelief.

I move forward and he looks at me with a tortured

expression.

'I'll leave you two alone,' Billie says and walks quickly to her room.

'We have to talk,' I say.

'There is nothing to say,' he replies. His eyes are burning in his face, though. There is something he wants to say. Badly.

'Tell me,' I urge.

'I am leaving for Africa soon. I volunteered. I'll be working for a medical charity.'

I gasp. There are already tears prickling the backs of my eyes. 'Where in Africa?'

'Sudan.'

'For how long?'

He shrugs. A half smile. The old Jack poking through. 'Until I feel better, I guess.'

I nod. I'm not going to cry. I'm going to be strong for him. Make it easy for him. I'm going to wish him well.

'Before I go will you…kiss me, Lana?'

My mouth gapes. I stare at him. First thought: I love Jack. I can't refuse him such a small thing. Second thought: my mouth belongs to Blake. I think of Blake saying, 'I don't share.'

'Forget it, forget it,' he says, and whirling around makes for the door. For a few seconds I am frozen, and then I am running out of the door calling to him. He turns in the corridor and looks at me.

'Yes,' I whisper.

I owe him this. This is my Jack. He would give his life for me. I love him. I have loved him all my life. One parting kiss. What harm can it do? The kiss is already doomed.

He strides towards me, broad-shouldered, confident, sure. The old Jack in every line. He stops in front of me. I look up into his bright blue eyes, totally different from Blake's or mine. 'Old blue eyes,' my mum used to call him. He could have had any girl. All the girls in school used to call him Mr. Happening and he was in love with me the whole time.

He puts his hands on either side of my cheeks, butterfly light. There is no fire in his eyes. There is no lust. There is only the light of love, such love that the breath catches in my throat. It pours out of his eyes, drowning me, leaving me speechless, parting my mouth. He smells of soap and some cheap aftershave. But clean. And good. And wholesome.

Gently, gently his lips descend.

And when they arrive I tremble at the surprise that is Jack. All my life he has constantly surprised me, by the unfathomable depths of him. Like that time he was shirtless and turning on himself like a wild animal, growling 'Who next?' to his attackers. He is truly unknowable.

His kiss begins gently and without any hope, but there is such skill and technique that on a purely physical level my body begins to react to him. *Where did you learn to kiss like this?* My shocked mind wonders distractedly. And suddenly I am not standing in a concrete corridor in a council block of flats kissing my brother. I am making love to a beautiful, surprising man who is in love with me, and who I could have fallen in love with if only he had kissed me like this a year and a half ago.

Shit, what the hell am I doing?

I put my hands on his chest to push him away. Immediately he moves back.

'Why didn't you tell me?' I whisper.

'I didn't think you were ready,' he says bitterly, and begins to walk away.

'Jack.'

He turns slightly.

'Please take care of yourself.'

He doesn't answer. Simply walks away. I watch him until he disappears down the road. Then I gently shut Billie's front door and begin to walk. Sorab will be safe with her for a few hours. I don't have a destination. I simply walk in the general direction of St. John's Wood. I feel ripped apart. I truly never suspected. Now he is going to a dangerous war-torn country and he may never come back. I don't know how long I walk, but suddenly I am very close to the apartment and mind-numbingly tired. I cannot face the walk back to collect my son. I realize my mobile phone and my handbag are in the pram.

I find a phone box and make a collect call to Billie and she agrees to keep Sorab for another hour. I will go back to the apartment. Rest for half an hour and then go back to Billie's. I wave to Mr. Nair and go into the lift. In the lift I sag against the wall. I used to be able to walk for miles and never feel this tired. Billie is right. I am only a shell of what I used to be.

I open the front door of the apartment and Blake is standing in the corridor. I stop and stare at him. Why is he home? There is an expression on his face that I have never before seen.

In a flash he crosses the room and closes the door. He bends his head to kiss me and rears back as if burned. His eyes blaze into mine. Then things happen so fast they are blur to my tired mind. He grabs me by the upper arms and the next moment I have been lifted off the ground and I am lying dazed and flat on my back with him crouching over me like a predator, his eyes so ferocious I do not recognize them. He pulls my skirt up and tears my knickers open. Then he grabs my legs by the kneecaps and opens them wide. He jerks his face between my legs, and to my eternal horror, *sniffs* me. Like an animal.

I am so shocked and humiliated, I freeze.

When he raises his head and looks at me I am staring at him, speechless, horrified. The wild, aggressive expression on his face is gone as quickly as it had come. I look at him almost in disbelief. *I have just seen him lose control.* I find my strength, my fight, and raising myself on my elbows, I place my feet on the carpet and push hard and away from him. He grabs my foot. I kick out with the other. He grabs that one too and pulls me toward him. I slide helplessly along the carpet, like a rag doll towards him.

'Don't,' he growls. 'I smelt a man on you.'

I am flat on the ground. His face is very close to mine. I close my eyes. 'I kissed Jack.'

'Why?'

'Because he is leaving for a war-torn country. Because I may never see him again. Because he asked me. Because he has never asked me for anything before,' I sob. The tears are running down my temples into my hair. I feel shocked and bruised. I am in love with a man who wrestled me to the ground and sniffed my sex organs for the smell of another man. Another man's scent on me has brought out dormant territorial and protective instincts in the cool banker. The instincts are destructive, feral.

He scoops me up in his arms 'Shhh... I'm sorry, I'm sorry. I didn't mean to frighten you,' he croons.

But I cannot stop crying.

'Please don't cry. You didn't do anything wrong. I just can't bear thinking of you with anyone else. I don't even want you in the same room with other men,' he confesses.

'What is happening to us, Blake?' I whisper.

'Nothing is happening to us. I just lost my head for a moment. I didn't think. It was pure instinct.'

'What's going to happen when the 42 days are up, Blake?'

He looks pained. 'I don't know, but will you trust me

that everything I do is in your best interests?'

'And what is in my best interest, Blake?'

He sighs heavily. 'In thirty-one days you will know.'

Softly he starts kissing my eyelids, my cheeks. He ends on my mouth. He kisses it hard, forces my lips open and lets his tongue sweep into my mouth. Possessively, staking claim on what is his, erasing the mark, even the memory of the other man's mouth. His hands are unbuttoning my blouse, cupping my breasts. I am lifted and the bra clasp flicked open. The blouse is being pulled out of my skirt. It slips easily from my shoulders. The skirt follows.

We have sex on the floor beside the front door. The shock and the pent-up emotion make the climax explosive, and afterwards, I feel so exhausted I wish I could sleep where I am. He picks me up and carries me to the bed.

'I have to go and pick Sorab up from Billie,' I whisper.

'Tom is already on his way. Sleep.'

I sleep for many hours. When I wake up it is 7:00 pm. I see the light from beneath the connecting door of Sorab's room. I pull on a dressing gown and pad towards the door. I open it and stand for a moment unnoticed. Bands of steel around my heart. Blake is holding Sorab in his arms and rocking him. I have denied Sorab a father. I have denied Blake his son. I had never thought to see Blake so domesticated. He looks up and smiles.

'Ah, you are awake?'

I smile.

'Did you sleep well?'

'Yes, thank you,' I say, but I did not. These days I wake up unrefreshed, tired. I hope I am not sickening for something. 'Here, give him to me. He probably needs to be changed by now.'

'No need, all done.'

'You changed his nappy?'

'It's not exactly rocket science.'

I go to Sorab and put a finger into the nappy around his belly. The nappy is perfectly snug. He has done a good job.

'When did you learn to put a nappy on a baby?'

'I watched you.'

'Hmnnn... I guess I'd better prepare some formula for him.'

'No, need, I just fed him.'

'Quick learner, aren't you?'

'Like you wouldn't believe,' he says and grins, all boyish and gorgeous. As if I have not seen him tackle me to the ground and smell my sex for the scent of another man.

He puts Sorab into my surprised hands. 'I hope you are hungry. Dinner will be served in half an hour.'

'Starving,' I say to his retreating back.

The wine is an old vintage from the Barrington estate in France, the steaks are perfectly juicy and tender, and the salad is out of a bag, but perfectly dressed and salted.

I gaze wonderingly at him as he sits opposite me in a black shirt, faded blue jeans and bare feet. Like you wouldn't believe, indeed.

He learnt to cook while we were apart!

Twenty

Billie calls surprisingly early in the morning. She has something to tell me.

'What is it?' I ask.

'Tell you when you get here,' she says, her voice full of something delicious, something she can barely keep suppressed.

I hurry over. When I arrive with Sorab she is in the bath.

'In here,' she calls. I go and sit on the toilet seat. There is glittery-green eyeshadow on her eyelids.

'Gosh, you look like you've had a fun night.'

She grins widely. 'I went to The Fridge last night.'

'Who with?'

'On my own.'

I frown. 'Why?'

'Just wanted to.'

'Well?'

'I let a man pick me up.'

'What?' I am so surprised my mouth actually hangs.

'What can I say? This huge man, I mean really big, with muscles coming out of his ears, came up to me and told me that the tattoos on my neck were the most beautiful things he had ever seen.'

I giggle.

'All right. It is possible that he has cornered the market on going up to girls and complimenting the very thing that everyone else has told them is ugly. But nobody has ever thought my tattoos are beautiful. Not you. Not even Leticia. And it made me curious about him.'

'But you don't fancy men.'

'I know. "Thanks, but I'm a dyke, mate," is what I told him too.'

'And?' I prompt.

'"That's only because you haven't been to bed with me yet," he said, and I was so high, I was actually impressed with that level of arrogant confidence. "I'll fuck you, but I'm not sucking your dick or doing anything else gross like that," I replied.'

'Billie!' I squeal.

'No point being coy. I'm not sucking any man's dick. Anyway, "I'm not too keen on that practice either," he said, so we went back to his place.'

'And?' I can barely believe what I am hearing.

'And it was actually very exciting. You know how I always take control. He wouldn't let me. He was very strict and masterful, and fucking strong too. I've never had anyone so...well...authoritative in bed before. It was something new, something I'm not used to.'

'So you enjoyed sex with a man?'

'I hate to say yes, it messes with my self-identity, but yeah. In the morning he brought me breakfast, ugh, sausages and eggs.'

I am almost laughing. 'What did you do?'

'I ate it.'

'What?'

'Wasn't bad.'

'Billie, you haven't had a proper breakfast since you were two!'

She laughs.

'Are you going to see him again?'

'Maybe. He took my number, but he's going to be away for a month. If I see him again, I see him again; if I don't, I don't.'

'But you want to...'

'Yeah... I guess I do. There's something intriguing about him.'

'Does this mean you are no longer a lesbian?'

'Don't get me wrong. I still fancy you more than him, but maybe I'm not just DC but AC too.'

'What's his name?'

'Rose, Jaron Rose.'

I bite my lip. 'Actually, I have something to tell you too.'

'Get on with it then.'

'I don't want you to freak out but...'

'I won't freak out. What is it?'

'Victoria's mother came to see me.'

'Bloody hell. That was quick. Let me guess. She warned you to leave Blake alone?'

'Yes, she did warn me, but the funny thing is, I think she thought she was warning me for my own good.'

Billie snorts disbelievingly. 'You're soft in the head.'

'Just hear me out, OK?'

'I'm all ears.'

'It was all very vague and mysterious, but basically she told me I was in danger.'

'Now you *are* freaking me out. What kind of danger?'

'She didn't say, but something about the way she said it made me realize that she was frightened. She shouldn't have come to see me. She came against her better judgment.'

'So what exactly did she say?'

'She said I should beware of Cronus.'

'Who the hell is that?'

'I didn't know either. But he is the god of time. Usually depicted as an old man with a grey beard. According to Greek mythology Cronus deposed his father and, in fear of a prophecy that he would suffer the same fate, he began to swallow each of his children as soon as they were born.'

'Charming. What's that got to do with you?'

'I don't know. I'm trying to work it out.'

'Why don't you ask Blake?'

'Because she said, don't trust anyone and I'm not sure
—'

'You don't trust Blake!' Billie's eyes are huge with shock.

'It's not that I don't trust him. I trust him with my life, but he is definitely hiding something important from me. Besides, he has already told me that the less I know the safer I will be.'

'Jesus, Lana, what kind of shit are you messed up in?'

Twenty-one

I wake up exhausted.

In fact, last night I was so dead to the world, I did not even wake up at dawn to take care of Sorab. Blake did. Before he left for work he gently shook me awake and said, 'Shall I ask Gerry to come take care of Sorab today?'

But I had shaken my head. 'No, I'm fine.'

'OK, I'll call you mid-morning.'

I pull myself out of bed. I am so tired I feel almost tearful. I hear Sorab cry and I move instinctively towards the sound. I pick him up and put him in his playpen. He looks at me with his great big blue eyes and grizzles softly. I know what he wants. He wants me to carry him. But I can't. Not today.

Today I just want to go back to bed and sleep. I wipe my hand down my face. I go over to the tin of biscuits. Flavored with organic grape juice they are his favorite. I thrust one into his hand. He starts nibbling on it and I stumble out of the room. I have a plan. I will leave him with Billie and I will have a good sleep. I need it.

By the time I reach Billie I actually feel dizzy.

'What's the matter with you?' Billie says.

'Tired,' I say. 'Can you just watch him while I go back and sleep for a few hours?'

'Whoa,' she says. Her voice sounds far away. 'You're going nowhere like this. Come here.'

Obediently I turn towards her voice. She leads me to her bed. I fall gratefully into it; it smells of her hairspray and perfume. Familiar. I turn my face towards it.

I feel a cool hand on my forehead. 'Shit,' I hear her say. 'You're burning up with fever.'

I go to sleep and when I wake up I hear Blake's voice, raised, angry.

'Why didn't you call me?'

'It's not like she's dying. She's got the fucking flu. Everybody gets it.'

'I'm calling the doctor.'

'Who's stopping you?'

I feel Blake sitting on the bed beside me. He seems odd, distressed.

'I'm all right. It's just the flu.'

'The doctor will be here soon.'

The doctor confirms Billie's diagnosis. 'Flu, but,' he cautions, 'she does seem malnourished. Perhaps even anemic. I'd recommend a full check-up.'

Other doctors come and inject me with cocktails of

vitamins, C, B complex. I must admit I feel better after these injections. I am spoon-fed tomato soup that Laura has sent. It doesn't taste anything like the canned Heinz tomato soup that I am used to. I make a face.

'It's just missing the MSG,' Blake comments dryly. He makes me finish it all.

I am then moved into my old room. The sheets have been changed. They feel cool against my skin. It is a relief to fall into soft blackness, but I sleep badly. Tossing and turning through the night. Sometimes I open my eyes and Blake is always there. Awake and working. He has brought a desk into my room. The fever breaks in the early morning hours. I sit in bed and eat a cup full of jelly. The jelly tastes funny. I complain and grumble.

'You are such a terrible patient. Get it all down. It is all good stuff. You're body is crying out for minerals and vitamins,' Blake scolds.

To my absolute horror I am put into a wheelchair the next day and wheeled down the corridor and into the lift. It stinks of urine and I see Blake's mouth settle into a hard line. He hates dirt, chaos, disorder, ugliness.

For a week I am invalid, but the expensive daily injections and cups of red, green and yellow jelly are useful, and soon I am almost myself. My appetite returns and I feel good again.

But I have lost five days of my 42.

Twenty-two

I meet Blake for lunch in Maide Vale, in a restaurant that reflects the laid-back style of the area.

'Why are we meeting here?' I ask.

'Got something to show you,' he says.

'What?' I ask curiously. His eyes are twinkling, he laughs at my impatience.

'Why spoil the surprise?'

'OK.'

After lunch, Tom drives us to an apartment block in the middle of Little Venice. We get out and take the lift to the fifth floor. Blake fishes a key out of his pocket, and with a lopsided smile at my uncomprehending frown puts the key into the door and opens it. We step into an empty apartment. I am immediately drawn to the balcony. It has a wonderful view of all the waterways and canals that make up Little Venice. Pretty amazing.

'Do you like it?'

'Yeah,' I say carefully, not sure where this is going. And then suddenly it hits me. This is my kiss-off present at the end of our 42 days. I keep a bright smile on my face, hope it doesn't look too false, and turn around.

He has taken Sorab out of the pram and is coming towards me with him in his arms. 'He'll drool all over your suit,' I say, trying to appear normal.

'Come, I'll show you the rest,' he says. He seems almost excited. That kind of annoys me. I remember Jack saying, no man wants a woman for just 42 days. You'll end up as his mistress.

Silently, I follow him around the two-bedroom flat. The main bedroom is sunny and spacious, but my heart is breaking inside. He wants to stash me away here!

'Do you think Billie will like it?'

'Billie?' I ask, confused.

He nods. 'You know her taste, do you think she will like it?'

I frown. 'Why?'

'It's for her.'

'What?' I laugh. A crazy cackle.

'Well?'

I laugh again with relief. It is tumbling inside me like an upturned bowl of marbles. The sound a joy to behold. 'She'll love it.'

'That's settled then,' he says, in a satisfied tone. 'It is in your name, of course, since I know that she keeps... er...complicated financial arrangements with the Her

Majesty's government, but whenever she becomes financially independent you can transfer it into her name.'

'Why are you doing this?'

'I don't want you visiting her on that horrible estate. Every time you tell me you are going there I almost break out in hives.'

I can't stop smiling.

'Obviously it needs a new bathroom and kitchen, but you girls can redecorate it in any way you want. Just liaise with Laura and she will open accounts wherever you want.'

I am so full of joy I am almost in tears. 'It is the most wonderful thing that anyone has ever done for Billie.'

He becomes suddenly brusque with embarrassment. 'Well, I have to get back to the office. Tom will drop you off wherever you want to go. See you at home this evening.'

I throw my arms around his neck. I feel so much love for him I am almost in tears. 'Thank you,' I whisper. 'Thank you so much.' I pull back and look deeply into his beautiful eyes. 'I really, really, really love you, you know. With all my heart.'

He bends his head and kisses me tenderly. Why won't he tell me he loves me? I know he loves me. Someone who is not in love could never do something this generous and delicious.

I go with him to the door. He stops. 'Who did you think the apartment was for?'

'Me.'

'You?' He seemed genuinely confused. 'Why would you think that?'

'I thought it was my kiss-off gift.'

He caresses my cheek with the back of his hand. 'You have no idea at all, have you? The papers are on the ledge over the fireplace,' he says, and then he is gone.

I stand in the balcony and watch him leave the building, cross the road and get into the back of a waiting dark blue Rolls-Royce with a silver hood. Then I call Billie.

'Billie, what are you doing right now?'

'Watching my nails dry.'

'Can you get a cab and come meet me in Maida Vale.'

'Why, what's in Maida Vale?'

'Do you want to spoil the surprise?'

'Why would I wanna do that?'

The bell rings in less than half an hour.

I open the door with a stupid grin on my face. I can't help it. I am so happy and excited for Billie.

'I've smeared my nail polish so this better be good,' she says, waving her ruined nails in front of my face.

'Sorry,' I say and she steps over the threshold. Just like me she goes immediately to the balcony.

'Wow, this is some view, isn't it? Whose place is it?'

'Yours.'

She turns around slowly. 'Sorry?'

'It's yours. Blake bought it for you.'

'For me?' She is frowning.

'Yup.'

Her eyes are narrowed. 'Why?'

'I think he hates Sorab's godmother to live on a council estate. He was kind of put off by the syringes and the smell in the stairwells.'

'What do you mean by *for me*? What happens when your 42 days are up?'

'You still get to keep it.'

She breaks into a mad grin. 'A flat right in the middle of classy Little Venice just for little ole me? Wow. You know what, if he hasn't been straight as a die in all his dealings with you from the moment he met you, I'd never believe it.'

'Well, it's in my name at the moment, but as soon as our business picks up and you stop being on the dole, I'll transfer it into your name.'

I hand her the papers.

She looks at them. 'Wow, who'd have thought?' She lifts her face to mine. There are tears in her eyes. She blinks them away proudly.

I smile at her. 'And you know what is even more exciting? Blake has agreed to pick up the decorating tab. You have carte blanche to decorate it in any way you want.'

'I just don't know what to say, Lana,' she says suddenly.

'Is it worth messing your nails for?' I tease.

'Can you put that child down for one moment,' she asks gruffly.

I put Sorab into his stroller and she envelops me in a bear hug. 'Thank you, Lana. I know you don't pray, so every day I get down on my knees and I pray that everything will work out for you,' she whispers in my ear.

I pull back. 'You do?'

She nods solemnly.

'Thank you,' I say, and smile. Grateful that she is my friend.

Twenty-three

He made me lie on the bathroom floor and gave me a hot coffee enema. Twice he administered it. It was uncomfortable. And twice I sat on the toilet until there was no more to void, and I felt strangely light and cleansed.

At the edge of the bed he pushed me back and holding onto my thighs he spread my legs wide and pinned them on either side of my head. My lower body rolled up to accommodate his needs. Now nothing was hidden from his eyes. Completely exposed to him, I looked into his hooded eyes,

He laid his palm on my open sex.

'You are very damp,' he said, and immediately

after sank into my wet cunt.

He buried himself deeper still. I cried out, but he only said, 'You were made for me. This body was made to take me and only me. When I am finished with you there will be no part of your body that I will not have been in or on. Every fucking inch of you is mine and mine only.'

He pulled out of me and without taking his eyes off me smeared his thumb with lubricant.

'Now lie down on your face and present yourself to me.'

I turned over and lay down with my cheek flat on the mattress and my butt rounded and pushed up towards him.

'Spread your legs more for me.' I obeyed and he slowly inserted his thumb into the ring of clenched muscles.

'I own this,' he said, dipping it in and out. In and out.

Strange, but not painful. Pleasurable even. I knew what he was doing. He was stretching me. Touching the sensitive walls, pressing on vital nerve endings until my body began to move restlessly on the bed. Now he knew I was excited and ready.

He covered his erection with jelly and began to press it against me.

This time I cried out in protest. A sharp, unfamiliar pain. A frisson of panic in my lower belly. He is too big. I won't be able to take him.

'You have to relax,' he said. 'Let me in... Pain has possibilities, holds a different kind of pleasure.' His voice was low, seductive.

I wanted to take him in, but my muscles remained clenched, uncooperative. He could not have moved an inch further.

'You have to trust me, Lana,' he said and reaching under me began to stroke my clitoris. I began to tremble. Taking advantage of my distracted state, he pushed suddenly into me.

The pain was immediate and sharp, and I screamed out, but he had become motionless, to allow my body to absorb the foreign intrusion, the strange sensation of hot fullness. When he judged my body had come to accept him, he pushed all the way in.

I moaned restlessly.

There was still pain, but more than the pain was the pleasure of being taken by him. In that position that I should have considered debased and humiliating I found decadent pleasure.

He began to move inside me and I couldn't help the strange animal sounds that came out of me. Firmly gripped by my rectum and the foreignness of what we were doing he came fast, spilling his seed deep inside me, crying out my name. He buckled against me, but he did not pull out of me. Instead he reached over and began pleasuring my clit.

'Clench your muscles,' he said and I obeyed.

The unfamiliar sensations of pressure and pleasure coursed through my body. I climaxed, shaking and trembling, as quickly as he had. For some time he remained inside. When he pulled out of me I was sorry. I wanted him back inside me. He belongs inside me.

Every part of me cries for him when he leaves.

I put the pen down and close my journal. Nowadays, I write without resentment, eagerly, because it is the only real and honest communication I have with him. I feel him distant. Moving away from me. Something is bothering him. The days pass away in a haze of sex—it seems to me more like a desperate desire to physically meld with me, to forget for a while whatever is troubling him.

Once he woke up, drenched in sweat, shouting hoarsely, almost sobbing, 'Not her, please.'

When I touched him, he turned to me with wild eyes, and recognizing me, fell into the crook of my neck gratefully, and hugged me so tightly, I whimpered. But when I asked him about his nightmare, he whispered in my ear, 'Just don't ever leave me.'

As if I would ever leave him. As if it was me that set a limit of 42 days on our time together.

Twenty-four

Billie calls. She wants me to drop Sorab off for the afternoon. She is lonely. She misses him. I leave Sorab with her and go to Sloane Square. I want to buy a pink shirt for Blake. It's a sort of joke. He thinks pink shirts are sissy, and I think they are a turn-on—only really macho men can carry them off. I find the shirt I want and I am about to return home when I suddenly stop in my tracks.

Rupert Lothian.

There are two men with him, business types in dark suits. He must have just had lunch with them. For a moment we are both so surprised neither of us speaks, but he is first to recover.

'What a lovely surprise,' he says smoothly, and lays a heavy, proprietary hand on my arm. And grasps it. I try to shake him off unobtrusively, but he tightens his hold. He turns to the two men and tells them he will call them later. They call out their goodbyes and leave together, and Rupert turns his attention to me.

'I was wondering, just the other day, what the devil happened to you. How've you been, gorgeous?'

'I'm fine, but I'm late and I really must be going. It was nice to see you again, though.'

'What's the rush? Come and have coffee with me,' he invites. His voice is genial and wheedling, but I still have the memory of his oyster-flavored saliva pouring down my throat, his finger digging into my crotch, seeking rough entry. If only I am big enough and strong enough to be able to say, 'Don't stop, don't look at me, don't touch me. Walk on by.' But I am not big enough and I remember the sheer male strength of his rugby player's hands as he pinned me against the wall and abused me.

'Perhaps some other time.' I take a step back, but he refuses to relinquish his hold on my hand. 'Are you still with him?'

'That's really none of your business.'

'As a matter of fact, I am looking for some business. Are you available? Same terms as before.'

I twist my arm and try to wrench it free, but his grip is like an iron clamp. The fury that I never expressed before rises like bile inside me. Without thinking I bring my other arm up and hit him, and instantly he lets go of my arm, and throws a punch in my direction. It should have hit me square in the face, but it only glances my chin. I stare in surprise as he lands on the ground. Flat on his back. Out cold. I look up dazed. A man is standing in front of me. I stare at him. The blood thrums in my ears.

'Are you all right?' he asks solicitously. He is looking at my chin.

'Yes, I think so.'

'Good. You best be on your way, then.'

'What about him?' I glance at Rupert, sprawled, unmoving. He could even be dead for all I know.

'Don't worry about him. I'll make sure he is all right.'

I nod, but the whole thing is surreal. The speed with which this man arrived on the scene and the swift, totally professional move that floored a huge man like Rupert. I look again at the man. He has sandy hair, a fit, wiry body and flinty eyes. Dressed in a black shirt, leather jacket and blue jeans, he could be anybody off the street, but I know he is not. He did not appear here by accident.

His kindness is a mirage. Pay him the right money and he will just as easily break my neck. I take a step away from him.

'Don't forget your shopping,' he reminds me politely.

I turn and look at the shopping bag lying on the sidewalk. The pink shirt is poking out. I pick it up and without a word, without thanking him, I walk away quickly. As if I am running away from the scene of a crime. Perhaps I am.

I walk for God knows how long, my mind in turmoil. I come upon crowded walkways where people brush past me, but I feel nothing. When it finally dawns on me, I come to a dead stop suddenly. A woman runs into me and swears inelegantly. She loses her anger when I turn around to apologize. She looks at my chin, mumbles something and walks on.

I walk towards the wall of a building and lean against it.

Finally, one more piece in the mad puzzle. That is why Blake suddenly turned up at the apartment when Jack came to visit. And why he appeared so unexpectedly, his behavior so odd and secretive that day when Victoria's mother made contact and he suddenly whisked me away to Venice to hide, to think, and to regroup. And that too is how he knew to smell my face the day I kissed Jack.

He has always had me followed. The whole fucking time.

I feel angry and confused. Why? Why would he spy on me? He is so full of secrets. So mysterious.

By the time I reach the apartment I feel lost and unbearably sad. My entire life is a messy lie. Being secretly followed and watched seems an extension of all the other lies that my relationship with Blake entails. I open the front door and Blake comes striding towards me. Of course. He already knows about Rupert. I stand at the door and stare at him. His hair is disheveled, his tie has been pulled loose and is hanging a few inches away from his throat. But it is his eyes that I cannot look away from. I have never seen his eyes so wild with fear.

He lays a gentle hand on my throbbing chin. I flinch slightly. Immediately, he retracts his hand, and I swear I see tears swimming in his eyes. Then he pulls me into his arms and holds me tight. I hear him take a deep breath.

'I've been sick with fear. Where have you been all this time?' he asks in a hushed voice.

'I was walking.'

'Why did you switch your phone off?'

'I didn't. My battery was low. It must have died.'

'Oh God, Lana. Don't do that to me again.'

He takes a step away from me. 'He grabbed you. Did he hurt you anywhere else?'

I shake my head, but he pulls the sleeves of my coat and examines my arms. He touches the light bruises and looks at me. There is pain in his eyes. 'I have taken care of that bastard. He will never hurt another woman in his life again.'

I love you. I love you. I love you. I love you so much nothing else matters. But I don't say it. I can't. Something is very wrong. I cannot only think of myself. There is more than just me in this equation. There is Sorab. And I will love him the way my mother loved me. I will give him everything. And everything could mean no Blake EVER. Victoria's mother's words are still fresh. 'You and your son are in grave danger.' It would appear she was right.

I swallow the lump in my throat. I am in such pain I feel sick.

'What?' he asks worriedly.

'Nothing,' I say. But I actually feel dizzy. If he was not here, I would throw myself on the bed and howl—because I cannot have this man. I grit my teeth.

'Come,' he says and taking my hand leads me to the bedroom. His plan is simple. As Billie would say—he is a man, what can you expect? He wants me to sleep. When I wake up it will be all OK.

So I let him put me to bed. I watch him with blank eyes. I know he doesn't understand. And that he never will. Men are strong in a physical way, they don't know how to be strong in an emotional way. He thinks if I have no bruises I have no pain. I grasp his hand. 'Why did you have me followed?'

He runs his hand through his hair. He moves away from me. Paces the bedroom carpet like a caged creature. Then he sits beside me. 'Do you really want the truth, Lana?'

'Always.'

'Even if it makes a liar of you?'

'Even then.'

'Because I couldn't trust you with my son. Not in that horrible place you live in.'

My jaw drops.

'Jesus, Lana, what did you expect me to do? That place is crawling with drug addicts and low-lifes. I can't even bear it when you go there let alone a helpless thing like him.'

I gasp. 'You knew all along?'

'Oh, Lana, Lana, Lana. You must take me for such a fool. Did you really think I would not know he is mine? I knew from the moment I laid eyes on him.'

I am so shocked I can say nothing. Then I remember how silent he had suddenly become when he first looked at Sorab. And then he had blanked his eyes and casually asked me, 'Does he cry a lot?'

And that was the first day he had stayed the night. That was the first day he stopped drinking heavily and the first day he began to look at me without hate. It was the day he understood that I had left him not because I had been paid, but because I was pregnant. The next day his things had arrived and he had begun to live in the apartment with me.

'This elaborate charade... It was for you. For whatever you were playing at. I wanted to know what kind of woman you were. What kind of woman are you, Lana? You lie with me every night and you never think to tell me I have a son?'

I sit up. 'I was afraid.'

'Of what? Me?'

'I was afraid you or your family would take him away from me?'

'What are you talking about? I would never take him away from you.'

'It is in the confidentiality agreement I signed. If I have your child I will have to give it up.'

He sits on the bed and leans his forehead against his hand. 'This is all so fucked up.' He turns to face me.

'I'm sorry, Lana. I was so stupid.'

'What happens now?'

'Nothing. For now.'

A thought suddenly occurs to me. 'So you were having me followed because you are worried about Sorab's safety?'

He nods, but his eyes are careful, watchful.

'I didn't have Sorab with me today.' My voice is flat.

'You have your own detail. Do you think I would protect my son and not his mother?' His gaze is hard, uncompromising, refusing to be ashamed by his underhand methods.

'I don't like being watched. Call off my shadow?'

'After today? Are you kidding me?' He stands up and puts some distance between us. He turns to look at me. 'It's for your own protection, Lana.'

'Today was an exception. I don't need to be protected.'

'What's your real objection, Lana? It's not like it's in your face, is it? You didn't even know until today when Brian had to break his cover.'

'That doesn't make it better.'

His jaw clenches. 'I can't work. I can't concentrate. In fact, I think I actually go quite crazy when I don't know that you are all right. Can't you just humor me on this one thing?'

'Why are you so paranoid? Is there something that I should be fearful of?'

He comes to me. 'I have my reasons. You and Sorab

are my first priority.'

I look at him stubbornly.

'Is it really so much to ask, Lana?'

'OK.'

He breathes a great sigh of relief. 'Thank you.'

I touch his hand.

'There was a time I used think Arab men were mad to keep their women covered and hidden. Now I know where the need comes from.' He jabs his finger into the hard wall of his stomach. 'In here.'

God, I love this man so much it hurts. It actually hurts.

Twenty-five

I wake up in the cold, bluish light of dawn. For a moment I lie in the elaborately carved four poster bed confused by my surroundings, and then I remember. We are in Bedfordshire, at the Barrington's estate where Blake's sister lives. We arrived at the wrought iron electric gates in the dark, and ran up the curving stairs in the light from the moon. It was how I imagined young lovers of ancient times met, in secret and in the dark. We fell into bed and I ravished Blake after we had drunk a whole bottle of vintage champagne directly from the bottle.

I burrow into the delicious warmth of his body. He does not wake but puts a heavy hand on my stomach. I turn my head and smell the sheets. Starched sheets. My grandmother used to have starched sheets in her house.

Blake said I could explore the house and garden as long as I keep away from the west wing, where his sister lives.

And now I long to go into the extensive garden. I lift Blake's hand and edge out from under it. The morning air is surprisingly chilly. I dress quickly. There is a large extra blanket folded at the foot of the bed. I throw it over my shoulders and slip out of the room. The entire house is dim and silent. I walk down the corridor and stand at the top of the beautiful staircase. I am drawn to a painting.

A family at breakfast scene. Probably Victorian. I go closer to it. A man with rosy red cheeks is spooning egg into his mouth; some of it is dropping off his spoon. He is holding the egg cup very close to his chin. I realize that it is not a picture that is meant to depict the family as dignified or grand, but is a parody of unparalleled and uncouth greed. It is also ironically a celebration of greed.

My hands glide down the polished banisters.

I try to imagine Blake as a boy running in these spaces as I pass the music room with its priceless antique furniture, its rare objets d'art, and its tables of exotic orchids and feel a kind of lingering sadness. Nothing truly happy has happened in this house. Not even the children who ran through these rooms were happy. The entire house is crying out for the sound of laughter.

I pass another room where the heavy drapes are still shut and enveloped in the same sort of despairing gloom. Through that room I can see the main reception room. In the foyer, which looks like the inside of a snail, hangs a Salvadore Dali, blue black with naked ritual dancers. It looks almost like an orgy to me. I cross the black and white checked marble floor and go out of the front door.

Outside it is warmer than inside the house. The sun is filtering through the trees. The vista is as magnificent as that of any old stately house. I walk around the side of the building, admiring the lay of the land. There I come upon a massive, industrial-size greenhouse. Flowers, vegetables, herbs and fruit are plentiful. Some reach the ceiling. In the middle of it is a large hydroponic pond.

At the side of the glass structure, I meet a peacock. I have never seen a peacock before and I slowly inch closer. Suddenly it opens its tail and I am shocked by how beautiful it is. A pure white peacock comes to join it. I wish it would open its tail too, but it doesn't. Instinct makes me look up and I see Blake standing at the door leading to the stone balcony outside the room we slept in.

He is looking at me.

I wave to him. He does not wave back, but opens the door and walks out onto the balcony. Shirtless, he stands looking down at me. I gasp at the sight. The way the house frames him, draws him in as part of it. I feel the privilege of his background swirl around him like an unseen hand and grasp him in its invisible clutches. He belongs here in these splendid surroundings. In every way he is different from me. I imagine what he must see. A woman wrapped in a blanket. I am not regal or imposing. I am the outsider.

After a grand breakfast Blake takes me to meet his

sister.

The reception room we wait for her in has been painted in soft pink. She is accompanied some a woman in a nurse's uniform and dressed in a long dress and blue sweater. A butterfly pin sits in her hair. Her eyes are as blue as Blake's, but otherwise she is nothing like him. Her brow is low and juts out and her skin is very pale.

'Hello, Bunny,' Blake says softly.

She drops her chin shyly and points at him.

'That's right. Your brother has come to see you. Isn't that nice of him?' the nurse says.

She nods vigorously.

'Would you like to show him your zoo?'

Again she nods and smiles.

'Perhaps you'd like to show him some of the tricks you have taught your animals to do.'

She beams with excitement.

Blake walks up to her. 'Will you show your animals to my friend too.'

For the first time her eyes come to rest on me. I smile. 'Hello,' I say.

She begins to rock her head and smile shyly.

'Come on then,' Blake says and holds his hand out to her.

She puts her pale hand into it, and we go outside towards a white marquee where there are seats all around it and a sandy enclosure in the middle. We take our seats and Elizabeth goes to the podium like structure at the entrance of the sandy enclosure. She claps her hand and a horse runs in. It gallops around the enclosure a few times and comes to a stop a few feet in front of her. She raises her hand and the horse rises to its hind legs and paws the air. She drops her hand and the horse ambles towards her. From her pocket she produces a cube of sugar and holds her hand out. The animal accepts the treat delicately and she turns around to smile proudly at us.

'Well done,' congratulates Blake.

Elizabeth claps her hands with delight.

I am truly amazed. It is very impressive to see a woman with the mental capacity of a child successfully train animals to perform tricks and obey her. Afterwards we watch Elizabeth's Indian elephant sit on a stool and turn around in a circle on his hind legs, a cute dog dance on command, and her pet monkey ride a bicycle.

When the show is over Elizabeth grabs Blake's hand and starts pulling him out of the tent. Blake gestures with his other hand for me to follow them. She takes him to her bedroom, a pink room filled with dolls, children's books and a rocking horse specially made to accommodate an adult. Taking a hairbrush from her dressing table she puts it into his hand and like a child runs eagerly to the bed and sits sideways on the edge of it.

At first Blake looks surprised that she should remember a ritual from so many years ago, but then he goes and sits behind her. With gentle hands he takes the butterfly clip out of her hair, and begins to brush her luscious, dark hair with long, sure strokes.

The girl clutches at his shirt and sobs, when it is time for us to go. She becomes hysterical when the nurse and a servant try to pry her away and they have to sedate her. In the car Blake is very silent and lost in his own thoughts. The way she had clung so desperately to him had distressed me too.

'It's great how she trained all those animals, though, isn't it?' I say, in an attempt to take him away from his unhappy thoughts.

'She doesn't train them. An animal trainer works with them and everybody just pretends that she has trained them.'

'Oh! Whose idea was it to do that?'

'My mother's.'

The brevity of his answer tells me not to go there. As ever, any talk of his family makes him clam up. I turn my head and gaze at the countryside and think of the fraught child locked away in that sad house, and the woman who won't acknowledge her child's existence, but who will go to elaborate lengths to create a private circus, which her daughter can ringmaster.

Twenty-six

I t is a Monday night. Blake has already phoned to say he will be late. He has a meeting. I am in bed reading when he comes in. He stands for a moment at the doorway simply looking at me. He seems different. Not so held together.

'What's the matter?' I ask.

'Just admiring your beauty.' Even his voice is drowsy and very appealing. This Blake is like nothing I know. He begins to walk towards me. Sits on the bed beside me and his liquored breath hits me instantly. I suck in my breath.

He nods knowingly, sagely. 'That's right... Been drinking.'

And then underneath the smell of the liquor, perfume. Expensive. Crushed flowers, herbs, musk. I have smelt this before. More than a year ago. When he came back from his birthday party. The realization hits me like a fist in the belly. Victoria. I stop thinking. Pain and fury are rushing into my brain. I raise both my hands and push him. He is not expecting such a reaction and he falls backwards, awkwardly, to the floor. I hear the thud of his body hitting the floor.

'What the fuck?' he slurs.

I fly towards his prone body and with quick hands I unbutton his fly and pull the trousers down to his hips. I tear furiously at his underwear. I bend my head and smell his crotch. But the odor is familiar. His. I sit back on my heels and look at him. He has raised his head off the floor and is looking at me, astounded.

'What's good for the goose... You were with a woman. I smelt her perfume on you.'

He lets his head drop to the carpet and sighs heavily. 'Yeah, my mother.'

Shit. Of course his mother was at the birthday bash last year too. I scramble over his prone body, and peer into his face. 'Ooops... Sorry.'

'Why don't you finish what you started, Lana?'

'Yes, sir,' I reply, and start tugging his trousers off.

'Take your clothes off and sit on me, but face my feet. I want to see my dick disappearing into you, and your pretty butt hitting my groin.'

I slip my nightgown off and ease myself on the hard column.

'Ride me hard and fast,' he says and I slam myself onto him.

'Oh yes,' he groans.

He is drunk and it takes longer than usual for him to come. By the time he does I am sweating and exhausted. I haven't come, but all I want to do is lie down beside him on the floor. I slide off him and am about to fall sideways to the floor when he catches me.

'I want you to rub yourself on my thigh until you come, but this time face me so I can see you come.'

I sit on his thigh, our juices squelching under me. The hairs on his thigh tickle me, and feel strange on my open pussy. I begin to rub myself on him while he watches me with avid eyes. The spasm of release comes quickly to my exhausted body. I slump against his body, my breast crushed against his rib bones, my cheek pressed on his chest.

'How could a woman who has had a baby have such a tight pussy?' His voice is rambling, sleepy.

I grin to myself. 'The woman doctor who delivered Sorab said she always puts in a couple of extra stitches. "For your husband" she said.'

Blake chuckles. 'That should be made standard practice.'

I rest my chin on his chest. 'Why did you get drunk today?'

He sighs heavily. 'Because today I had to make a very, very difficult decision.'

I raise my head up onto my palm and look into his eyes. 'Involving your mother?'

He brings a finger to my lips. 'Shhh...'

I sigh and drop my head back down. All these secrets.

Why can't he just trust me and tell me.

His voice is a whisper. 'It's a funny thing smell, isn't it? Do you know the thing I missed most after you left?'

'Sex?'

'Sex? I slept with hundreds of women.'

I feel searing pain at his words. 'In the beginning I had them all; brown, black, yellow, redhead, blonde, you name it. Got myself wasted and bedded them all. Then I began to be a little more discerning. They had to look like you, at the very least, from the back. If I drank enough and kept the lights dim, then I could fool myself that it was you, but the second I woke up, I knew: it was not you. They all—every single one of them—smelled of stale sex. No one had your smell. And I would practically run out of the door.'

His words, if they are meant to console or flatter me, have the opposite effect. I don't like the thought of all the women he has been with paraded before my eyes. Everything he has had with me he has had with others. There is nothing special just between us.

'Fuck my smell! Is there nothing we can do together that you have not done with anyone else?'

For a moment he simply looks at me as if pleading with me to recant. I don't. A bitter expression crosses his face. He sits up. Almost I can believe that he is no longer drunk, but stone cold sober.

'Get on the bed,' he says.

I obey immediately. This Blake reminds me too much of the old Blake. Far away and distant. Cold. A stranger. I am almost regretting my request. He gets up, goes to the drawer where all the sex toys that we never got around to using are kept, and pulls out a vibrator. This one is not big like the black and orange one that he humiliated me with. It is white, shaped like a missile, and of a modest size. He shrugs his shirt off.

'Lie down,' he says. His voice is clipped and quite scary. This is not my Blake. Yet, he is mine. This Blake lives inside the Blake that I know and I want this Blake too. This Blake is my opponent, but this Blake also holds secrets. Secrets that I want. I am not all light and he is not all dark. To be whole, to know him completely I only have to embrace his darkness and make it mine.

Do I have sufficient bravery?

Of course I do.

I will take my torch and go where love takes me.

He puts the vibrator on the bedside table close to him. Then he positions himself so his cock is over my mouth. And I note the most surprising thing of all. His cock is flaccid. This does not excite him in the least. He is doing this for me. Slowly, he lowers his dick into my mouth. I have never had it half-soft before and it is strange in my mouth. But it makes me determined.

I begin to suck so hard and so well and it grows quickly in my mouth to double its size. He takes the vibrator and inserts it into my slick vagina. He twists and turns it a few times inside the slippery walls, then removes it, and puts it into my hand. I take it, surprised. It is not switched on.

'Go on. Fuck me,' he orders.

But I am paralyzed. This is neither sexy nor erotic for me. I don't want to do it, and I can see in his eyes that this is unrelished territory for him. He takes my hand and, positioning it over his rectum, pushes my hand hard upwards. There is no real lubrication. Only the juices from my own sex. I see him jerk and wince with pain.

'Suck me and fuck me hard. Use both hands,' he commands, his voice clipped, foreign.

But I cannot. It is almost impossible for me to hurt him.

'Harder,' he growls, his eyes hard, unrecognizable. This time I obey. With both hands. As hard as I can. Only when I embrace his darkness… I see him straining with the pain and the undeniable dark pleasure. I know because I have already experienced it.

I suck so hard my lips and mouth start to hurt, but I know somehow this is very important. Once or twice he pushes so deep into my throat, I gag and choke. Finally, I see that he is near. He is coming. He starts to strain and clench. I increase my speed, and he is almost there. Always, at the point of climax he calls my name. This time he does not.

'Don't, Daddy,' he cries instead. His voice is high and strange, that of a frightened child.

I freeze, my mouth full of meat.

Twenty-seven

So does he, but the climax is greater than us; his horror, his shame, his secrets, his pride or my shock. He buckles as hot seed shoots into my throat. I extract the vibrator out of him, and he pulls himself out of my mouth. He is moving away from me. But I catch his hand. He stops, still on his knees, and looks down on me. Hauteur in every line of his face.

'Blake?'

'What?'

'I'm sorry.'

'Don't be. You wanted something I have never done with any other woman. You have it.'

'No, I mean about your father.' I still remember our conversation a year ago when he refused to condemn pedophiles, saying God made them that way and it was up to God to condemn them. 'Your father sexually abused you, didn't he?'

'My father didn't do it for sexual gratification.'

I frown. 'What do you mean?'

''He did it to cement his control over me.'

'What?'

'He has made me the person I am today. He had to teach me discipline. Our ways are different from yours.'

My mouth hangs open. Is he on the same planet as me? Teach him discipline? Our ways are different? 'What the fuck are you talking about, Blake?'

'You won't understand.'

'Damn right, I don't. Your father raped and brutalized you when you were a child, and you think that is a form of discipline?'

'My education was…vigorous and difficult, very difficult. I would not wish it upon anyone else, but without it I would not be fit to implement the agenda?'

'What agenda?'

'Without our banking services illegal drug trafficking would stop in a heartbeat. Without our economic policies there would be no poverty or starvation. Without our money wars would never be fought. By necessity we have to be cold and callous.'

For a few seconds my mind goes blank. These people are monsters who deliberate train their children to be monsters too. 'Did your father discipline your two brothers too?'

'Not Quinn.'

'Why not Quinn?'

'Quinn was never meant to lead. Only Marcus and I

will take over the helm of the empire.'

'Are you planning to do that to our son?'

'No. Never.' His eyes have become pained, but again, closed to me. The secrets are swimming on the surface. I cannot understand them. There is more. What the hell is he hiding?

I play my last card. 'Is your father Cronus?'

The change in him is so instant and so violent I can hardly believe my eyes. He crouches on all fours, like a cat, his face very close to mine, and his fingers flat against my mouth, but it is what is in his eyes that causes me to feel the first real frisson of crawling fear. They are desperately pleading with me as he shakes his head. I understand the silent plea. *Say no more.* I begin to tremble with real fear. What is it that is so terrible that it has put that expression into his eyes?

What dangerous secrets is my lover hiding?

I remember again when he said in Venice the walls are thin and might even have ears. He is still looking at me with that same expression of anxiety that I might decide not to obey his silent plea. When I nod slightly, he says coldly, callously, 'Meine Ehre heisst Treue.'

'What does that mean?'

'My honor is loyalty.'

And I know instantly that those words are not meant for me. The walls have ears. I frown. Trying to figure out what is going on. And then I grab my journal from the bedside table and scribble quickly on it.

Is this room bugged?

He shakes his head slowly and I understand that it is not an answer, but a reminder of his earlier plea. *Say no more.*

'I'm tired,' he says softly, 'and the worse for wear. Let's go to sleep.' He lifts his fingers off my lips.

'Yes, let's sleep. Things always look better in the morning,' I acquiesce, my voice shaky, barely a whisper.

He smiles at me. Gratitude. For what? Why? Then he kisses me on the mouth. 'Goodnight, my darling.'

'I love you,' I mouth silently.

He smiles sadly and covers our bodies with the duvet. I fall asleep with his body curved tightly around mine, but I sleep badly. Dreams, nightmares. All broken and disjointed. I am calling for him, but he has his face turned away towards strong winds and jagged rocks. Always I am frightened for him. It is never me in danger, but him.

I wake up when Blake suddenly jack-knifes into a sitting position. Dawn is breaking in the sky. 'I have to go to work,' he says.

'All right,' I feel very small and lost.

I stand at the door of the dressing room watching him get ready for work.

'Do you know that there are only ten days left?'

He eyes me in the mirror. 'Yes,' he says and carries

on knotting his tie.

'Coffee machine should be ready by now. Want one?'

'Thank you,' he says with a smile.

As I am putting the saucer under his espresso, Blake comes into the kitchen. Even today with my heart so heavy he makes my heart skip a beat. He looks a little pale, but he is so male, so gorgeous. I can almost forget what happened last night. That thin child's voice, begging Daddy to stop. I watch the movement his throat makes as he drinks his coffee. It is amazing to think that inside this accomplished totally confident man lives a damaged child, right down to the eerie little voice. But today is also different from any other day for a different reason. He is changed. I can feel it. Not in the way he feels about me, but inside him. A steely determination. He finishes his coffee and comes to me.

'What will you do today?'

'I don't know. Probably just mess about.'

He nods distractedly. Already he is elsewhere. Taken there by the steely determination. He kisses me. Then he opens his mouth as if to say something, but shuts it. 'Do you trust me, Lana?'

The little question is loaded with meaning. 'Yes, I trust you.'

He smiles tenderly. Then he is gone.

The day stretches ahead interminably. He will be gone for so many hours. I feel restless and oddly… frightened. I sit at the computer and Google Cronus. Is there something I have missed? A god who ate his own children. Father time. Another name for Saturn. What am I missing? I start delving deeper down the Google pages. Conspiracy sites churning nonsense start turning up.

I give up and type in 'Blake Law Barrington early years'. Nothing. There is not a single photograph or piece of news about him. I try to imagine him as a child. A little older than Sorab and suddenly tears appear in my eyes. Poor little thing. I have never come across it. Where a child who has been abused by its parent grows up to be a man and protects his abuser in such a loyal fashion. As if what his father had done was right. Did his mother know? The thought sickens me.

I don't understand what I am mixed up in.

I spend the morning and most of the afternoon wandering aimlessly around the apartment. The truth is I am stuck in an uncomprehending daze. I am even tempted to attempt contact with Victoria's mother. But the memory of that shrill look in her eyes frightens me. As if she is teetering on the border of madness. It is as if she is trapped in her own hell.

At four o'clock I hear the front door open. Blake is early. I run out gratefully to greet him. I have so missed him. I come to an abrupt stop in the middle of the corridor. It is not Blake standing just inside the door looking at me, but his father.

Twenty-eight

"The world is governed by very different personages from what is imagined by those who are not behind the scenes"

—Prime Minister Benjamin Disraeli of England, 1844

'Hello, Miss Bloom.'

'Hello,' I whisper.

'May I come in?'

'You are already in.'

His mouth twists haughtily. 'True.'

'Blake's not here.'

'I didn't come to see him.'

He passes me on the way to the living room, stops a few feet away, and prompts, 'Shall we?'

I follow. I am so furious with this man that my hands are white knuckled fists. I actually think I hate him. In fact, this is first human being I have met that I could feel all right about killing. This is the man who attacked a child and molded him into cold, money-making machine. But I know better than to order him out or to show my fury. I recognize that he is at the end of the maze I am lost in.

He stops in the middle of the living room. He does not sit and I do not offer him a seat. 'What do you want?'

'You have taken something very precious to me and I have come to ask you to give it back to me.'

I shake my head. 'I don't have anything of yours.'

'Don't play games with me, Miss Bloom. I haven't the time or inclination. I want you to leave my son.'

'What is it with you people? Don't you think Blake is old enough to decide who he wants to be with?'

'I've seen you. I've watched you beg my son to hurt you,' he says softly. But the venom in his calm words shocks me far more than if he had shouted at me. I take a step back. His cold eyes are unblinking. They watch me like a snake does its prey. He takes a step forward. 'This is the first time I have seen it. A woman begging a man to abuse her. I have to admit I enjoyed it even if my son didn't deliver. Next time you want to be hurt, ask me. I know exactly how to make you scream.'

I stare at him blankly. The walls not only have ears, they also have eyes, Blake. You didn't know that, did you? My mind scrambles for a way out of this nightmare. What has this man seen? He has witnessed me with my legs wide open, the black and orange dildo buried inside me. But I don't feel shame or humiliation. I feel fear. To beat down the fear, I simulate courage. I raise my chin to a fuck you stance.

'If you think your son shouldn't be with me, why don't you approach him directly?'

He looks at me strangely. As if I am a creature of very low intelligence that he is trying very hard to communicate with. 'Because I don't have to. I have what you want.'

'I'd rather die than take a penny from you.'

He smiles. 'I wouldn't insult you with money. You are far too subtle for that. Rather I am giving you another opportunity to be selfless and do something wonderful.'

I stare at him wordlessly as he weaves the net that he hopes to catch me with.

'I see a gloriously bright future for my son, but you are in the way. Your genetic imprint, your lack of education, your...your lack of social standing will eventually drag him down. What I am offering is a place in the countryside, near a good school, a beautiful home, a car, of course money, and introduction into better society than you have known.'

'I can't make that decision for Blake. He is old enough to choose what he wants.'

He holds up a hand. 'Let me finish. I know you are in love with my son. And believe me, that is something greatly in your favor. I know how difficult it must be for you, but the consequences if you do not leave him are enormous, incalculable...for Blake.'

'What do you mean?'

'If you don't leave him, I will destroy him.'

I laugh. A wild disbelieving laugh. 'You would destroy your own son just because he doesn't marry the woman you want him to.'

'What good is a son I have no use for?' he asks. His logic is so simple, so direct, so painfully sociopathic that I gasp.

'You wouldn't.'

'I would. I would destroy him in a heartbeat.'

'You can't.'

'Name me,' he says conversationally, 'a politician, a leader of a country, an important man in any sphere, and tomorrow I will turn him to nothing.'

'I'm not going to be responsible for destroying anyone so you can prove your power.'

'If you don't choose I will have to, and that will be a little less spectacular for you because then you can pretend that I had not the power to destroy, but only knowledge beforehand of something that was already in the pipeline. Choose anyone. Of course, I would prefer it if you did not pick prime ministers or presidents of countries. It is always expensive and time consuming to maneuver them into their positions of power—and they are all, other than one or two, being good little puppets at the moment, but if that is what it takes to convince you, then so be it. Or perhaps you would prefer a billionaire who particularly irritates you. Bill Gates? Warren Buffet?'

I shake my head. 'I'm not playing your game.'

'Fine, I will choose. The head of the IMF has been displaying a little less obedience than usual. I choose him. Tell me what kind of disgrace you would like to see come upon his unsuspecting head.'

'Nothing.'

'In that case let him be accused of rape. Not just any rape but the rape of a maid in a hotel room. Let her be of Asian descent. Thai would be too common. Would you be happy with Burmese?'

I say nothing. Simply stare at him.

'Now which newspaper do you choose to disgrace him?'

He is serious. He is actually going to ruin the career and life of an innocent man to make a point. I shake my head. 'I'm not going to be part of this.'

'What about the *Guardian*? Perhaps you'd like more than one newspaper to run the story? And a television channel? BBC? Or all of them?'

And suddenly my brain kicks in. He is bluffing. 'The BBC. I want the story to be run by the BBC,' I say. Surely he cannot have influence in the British Broadcasting Corporation!

But he smiles confidently. 'Done.'

I shouldn't have spoken. Now he knows he has me.

'When the story breaks tomorrow you will understand

the extent of my reach. I will do the same to my son. Here are the pictures that will grace the world media if you refuse to be reasonable.'

I realize that he has been holding an envelope all this time. He takes two steps towards me and throws it on the coffee table and it slides towards across and stops in front of me. He is so close now I notice his eyes. Eyes are usually called the windows of the soul, but in his case the windows are closed, or there is no soul to look out of them. There is not even a pencil of light from the empty interior.

I grasp the envelope with unsteady fingers. Photographs of me. With my hair tousled, my lips parted, my legs wide open. The photographs are clear and graphic. I look at them. The photos of that night when I taunted Blake into hurting me are so horrible I cannot go on. They do not reflect what really happened. They look like rape of the worst kind. I do not need to get to the end. I put them carefully back into the envelope and slide them back along the table top. My face is not flaming with embarrassment; it is numb with shock.

'No, keep them for your album,' he says.

Like a puppet I pull them back towards me.

'There are videotapes too of you and…other women. I'm afraid my son was rather indiscriminate when you left him the last time. They will be released a few days later on the Internet as supporting evidence. My son will become a common criminal. A sexual predator.'

I need to think. I am blank. My foe is too great. 'What happens if I agree?'

'You get to choose a leafy English suburb or if you prefer even another country. Perhaps you'd like to live in the sun.' I shake my head. 'No, well you get to choose. Somewhere like Weybridge, perhaps?'

'What will happen to Blake?'

'Absolutely nothing. He will mourn for you...for a while, then he will marry Victoria and have a family, and life will be good again.'

'What if he comes looking for me?'

'He won't know where to look. You will be fitted with a totally new identity. You'll have to give up your friends, of course. But you will make new ones, better ones.'

'Why are you going to so much trouble to keep me away from him?'

Something flashes in his eyes. So quickly it is almost as if in my numbed state I have imagined it. But it makes my skin go cold. It is not as simple as he makes it out to be. There is more. Much more.

I clasp my freezing cold hands together. For a moment neither of us speaks.

'There is another thing you must consider. My father was a banker, I am a banker, and my son will be a banker.
'

'What do you mean?'

'May I see my grandson?'

I understand immediately and the fear of before is

nothing compared to this. Oh God! He is referring to what he did to his son. He is implying that that is what Blake will do to Sorab.

'Blake will never do that to his son.'

'It is our way. If you choose to live in our world, then you must abide by our rules.'

I don't want this man anywhere near my baby. 'He is asleep,' I push through frozen lips.

'I will not wake him up. Just a quick peek,' he says with a sick, lizard smile.

Outmaneuvered I begin to walk stiffly towards the door. He follows me into Sorab's room. Protectively, I stand next to the crib. He stops a foot away from the crib and nods as if satisfied. Of what I do not know and do not ask. He turns away and I follow him, weak with relief, to the front door.

'Look out for the newspapers tomorrow morning. I will be in touch later in the day.' He opens the door.

'Mr. Barrington?'

He turns slightly towards me. 'Yes?'

'Who is Cronus?'

He turns fully towards me, and smiles. At that moment the strangest thing happens. Into those dead eyes climbs something. The most inquisitive look that you ever saw, an interest more avidly probing than you could ever have thought possible in those leaden eyes. It is as if it is no longer even the same man. A cold claw grips my insides.

'When you do your little Internet searches find the

shrouded one under the name of El,' he says and opening the door exits the apartment.

Twenty-nine

I do not walk, I run to my laptop to type El into Google's search engine.

El, I learn, is a deity dating back to Phoenician times. He is meant to be the father of mankind and all creatures. He is the gray-bearded ancient one, full of wisdom. The bull is symbolic to him. El is distinguished from all the other gods as being the supreme god, or, in a monotheistic sense, 'God'.

Through the ages he is listed at the head of many pantheons. He is the Father God among the Canaanites. In Hebrew text El becomes a generic name for any god, including Baal, Moloch, and Yahweh. Finally late in the text I come across the reference to Cronus.

Apparently it was the custom of the ancients during great crisis for the ruler of a city or nation to avert common ruin by sacrificing the most beloved of their children to the avenging demons; and those who are thus given up are sacrificed with mystic rites, arrayed in royal apparel and sacrificed on an altar. Those that follow this path are called the sons of El.

El the articles points out is the root word for elite.

I type in El and Cronus and learn that el cronus is a sex toy for men.

I type in Saturn and El and I find out that El is another name for Saturn. And Saturn is interchangeable with Cronus.

I sit back. To avert common ruin these men give the most beloved of their children as a sacrifice to their great god El. Did it mean what I thought it meant? That Blake's father would willingly sacrifice his son in exchange for more power?

I hear someone at the door and quickly click out of the pages I am on. I go to the door warily, but it is only Blake.

'Hi,' he says. He looks normal.

'Hi.'

'Everything all right?'

'Great.'

I walk up to him and kiss him. His kiss belies his casual attitude. It is the kiss of a man who is drinking sweet water from a fountain before a long journey into the desert. My hands entwine in his hair. I want the kiss to go on and on but my brain will not allow me to. Now that I have proof that walls have eyes and ears I cannot be myself. I withdraw my tongue slowly, work my hands down to his chest and give him a slight push.

He looks down at me, his eyes darkened and wild.

'Can we go out for dinner tonight?' I ask, forcing a smile.

'Sure. Where would you like to go?'

'That Indian place you took me to last year. I forget its name. The one named after the thieves' market.'

'Ah, Chor Bizzare.'

'That's the one.'

'We'll drop Sorab off at Billie's.'

'Shall we call Mrs. Dooley instead?'

'No,' I snap, and then quickly smile to take away the sting. 'Billie was just complaining that she never gets to see Sorab anymore.'

'OK.'

'Hey, I've always been curious. When you get your reports from your spies what do they tell you?'

'Just a list of your movements.'

'Have you received your report for today?'

'Yes, as I was on my way home.'

'What did it say?'

'Why?'

'Just want to know how it works.'

'OK. Today you stayed indoors until 3:50pm when you took Sorab out in the pram to the coffee shop around the corner. You had a cake and coffee and were back by 5:00 pm.'

I try hard to keep my face neutral. I never left the house!

Then it hits me. A look-alike lures the spy away and

the father enters the building and comes to see me. When the father leaves the look-alive re-enters the building. Now I know. Now I know. Blake cannot protect me, or himself, from his father.

His father has outsmarted him.

Thirty

"We are the tools and vassals of rich men behind the scenes. We are the jumping jacks, they pull the strings and we dance. Our talents, our possibilities and our lives are all the property of other men. We are intellectual prostitutes."

—John Swinton, Head of Editorial Staff, New York Times,
at a banquet thrown in his honour, 1880

Blake's father is true to his evil. *The Independent* and the *Guardian* are the first to report that the CEO of the International Monetary Fund, Sebastian Straus Khan, has been implicated in a scandal. A Burmese maid working at a hotel in New York has accused him of rape. He has been apprehended at the airport. The BBC runs the story at lunchtime. By evening every TV channel is running the story. There appears to be no investigation. Simply a story that is repeated almost word for word by all the different news feeds. Each one gleefully convinced of his crime.

That night when Blake comes home, I have painted my face and dressed in the sexiest outfit Fleur sent. The tight pink leather pants that Billie said, made my bum look all trapped and ripe and in need of rescuing, and a little top that leaves my shoulders and back bare.

His eyes light up. 'Wow, what's the occasion?' he breathes against my ear.

'We're not spending the night here,' I tell him. 'I've booked us into The Ritz.'

He smiles slowly. He has no idea. Inside I am dying. It is our last night together, a night I will never forget. We have dinner, I taste nothing, and then we go upstairs. There is champagne waiting in a silver bucket. I did not order it. Compliments of the house. I don't drink. I don't want anything to be fuzzy. I want to remember every last detail.

That night I am insatiable.

Again and again we make love until he says to me, 'Go to sleep, Lana, I don't want you falling ill on me again.' Even then I reach down and take his big, beautiful penis in my mouth and mumble, 'Use me for your pleasure. You have paid for this.'

And he looks deep into my eyes and says, 'Consider

the debt paid in full.' The irony stabs me in the heart. He has no idea.

When morning arrives, I pull him close and whisper, 'I love you. I'll always love you.'

And when he is leaving, he says, his voice husky with emotion, 'I'll miss you terribly until I see you again... tonight.'

And I almost break down. He will never see me again. Tears blur my eyes.

'Hey,' he calls very softly. 'Nothing can keep us apart.'

A sob breaks through. He does not understand.

When he is dressed and leaving, I hold on tight. He looks at me with strong, sure eyes. 'Nothing can keep us apart,' he says again. And then the door closes behind him and I sink to the ground. I cry as if I will break apart. When I am all cried out on the floor of The Ritz hotel, I rise numb, but ready. This is for him and Sorab. This will keep them both safe. I get into the lift, between my legs sore and the tips of my breasts singing from being sucked and bitten all night. Tom is waiting in the lobby for me. My thick coat is folded over his arm.

'Mr. Barrington had me get this from the apartment for you. It's a cold morning.'

Again I am struck by how carefully and thoroughly Blake's mind works. Always he is one step ahead. Except for the most important thing of all. I take off my light coat and get into the coat Tom has brought for me. I turn my head and notice a man looking at me. Our eyes meet. He does not drop his. I look away. The world has changed for me. A few months back I would have assumed that he found me attractive; now I am not certain if he has not been paid to watch me.

Outside an icy wind hits me. I am glad for the coat.

In the car I stare out of the window. I am actually in a state of shock. The thought of leaving Blake is so painful I refuse to think about it. It is almost as if I am on autopilot. There is an accident ahead and Tom takes the longer route through South Kensington. We pass an old church. The door is ajar and I jerk forward.

'Stop the car, Tom.'

Tom brings the car to a stop by the side of the road.

'I'm just going into that church.'

Tom looks at me worriedly. 'I can't park here.'

'I won't be long,' I say, and quickly slip out of the car. I go through the Gothic wooden doors, and it is as if I have stepped into another dimension. It is cool and hushed, the sound of the street outside strained out. The stonework is beautiful. I see the holy water, but I do not cross myself with it as my mother used to. I follow the gleam of candles into the belly of the church. There is no one else there. My footsteps echo in the soaring space. I go to the front of the church and sit on a wooden pew.

I close my eyes. I don't know why I came here. I don't believe in God. God has done nothing for me. All he has ever done is take and take and take every fucking thing I've ever had. I feel so incredibly sad and defeated

I wish I did not have to leave this quiet sanctuary. Hot tears are pricking the backs of my eyes. Life is so unfair.

Suddenly there is a gust of cold air. I open my eyes and look around. There is no one there. A draft? And then I have the strange sensation that my mother is there with me. I stand.

'Mum?' I call out.

My voice sounds strange and loud in that empty space.

'Mum,' I call out again, this time more desperately.

Nothing. I sit down again and close my eyes and presently the sensation returns that my mother is with me. The sensation soothes me. 'I love you, Mum,' I whisper. 'You left me too quickly. I never even had a chance to say goodbye.'

A feeling of peace settles on me. There are no words to describe the sensation. A timeless moment and I don't know how long I sit there. It is only the sound of footsteps that rouses me. I look behind me. Tom is standing by one of the pillars at the entrance. I stand up and go to him.

We walk silently to the car. There is a yellow parking ticket stuck to the windshield.

'Sorry,' I say.

'Laura will take care of it. My instructions are clear.'

We get into the car and Tom drives me to Billie's.

'Can we take a small walk down by the canal?' I say to her.

'What's wrong?'

I put a finger on my lips. 'I just fancy a walk.'

'All right,' she says, frowning.

'It's cold outside. Wear your coat.'

She takes her coat and follows me. When we are in the bracing air I tell her everything. Sometimes she will come to a sudden stop and stare at me mouth agape, and then I will take her arm into the crook of mine and we will continue on our path. I have never seen Billie look so white or totally robbed of her trademark wisecracks. It serves to highlight just how shocked I must be to be able to act so normally.

After the walk I kiss Billie's stunned face goodbye, and she pulls me hard against her body as if she could pass me some of her strength. Both of us know exactly how to contact each other. She is blinking back the tears.

'Be safe,' she calls as I push Sorab away from her.

Then I go home to await my next instructions.

When the call comes I leave my cellphone on the dining table and push the pram out to the front. I wave to Mr. Nair and he looks at me with confusion. I know that only a few minutes ago he must have seen my look-alike push an identical pram out of the door, perhaps to the coffee shop where she will have cake and coffee. Just outside the front door a car is waiting for me. A man jumps out of the front seat. I take Sorab out of his pram.

He holds open the back door while I slip into it. When I am settled in, he closes it with a gentle click. He folds the pram quickly, stores it in the boot, and gets into the front seat. Not a word has been exchanged by any of us. The car pulls away.

I think of my lookalike. She must have reached the patisserie by now. She has probably finished with her slice of cake. I imagine she must be an actress. Paid to play a part and then disappear. She will probably push her pram back into the building. Perhaps Blake's father has another flat where she can drop off the pram and effect a change of clothing. A hat, a scarf, a wig, before she exits the building forever.

And Blake, my poor darling love, will come home to his empty nest.

Thirty-one

We travel for many hours, stopping only at rest stops. Finally we arrive at a farmhouse in the moors. Here the countryside is wild and deserted. A strong wind is blowing as I get out of the car.

'Where are we?' I ask.

But the men simply smile politely. 'They will tell you when the time comes.'

Inside it is warm. A fire is already roaring in the fireplace. From the kitchen come delicious smells of roasting meat. I am shown to my room upstairs. It is pleasant enough, with blue patterned wallpaper and a double bed with a thick mattress. There is a crib in it too. As instructed I brought no clothes for Sorab or me. The man tells me everything I need is in the drawers and cupboards. I can already see the exact same brand of formula that I use for Sorab on the dresser.

He leaves and I go to stand by the window. The

moors seem to stretch into the horizon. Not a single dwelling in sight. Fear gnaws at me. Why am I here? I know Blake's father said this is to be my temporary home until everything is arranged, but something feels very wrong.

Another voice in my head frets, *you didn't keep your promise to Blake*. But I had no choice. I protected Blake with my own body. I walk away from the window and lie down on the bed, curling my body around Sorab's sleeping one. I close my eyes and pretend I am in my bed in St. John's Wood until there is a knock on the door.

'Dinner is ready,' someone informs.

I wash my hands and freshen up before going downstairs. I put Sorab in the playpen and one of the men puts a plate of food on the table and withdraws from the room. I hear him open the front door and go outside. I eat alone. The food is wholesome and steaming hot, and I finish it all. Something tells me I am going to need all my strength.

I fall asleep while I watch TV in my room.

I am awakened by a hand over my mouth. My eyes jerk open. A man's voice urgently whispers, 'Please don't make any noise.' A small torch is switched on. 'Blake sent us,' and he dangles over my eyes, in the light of the torch, the ruby and black diamond necklace that Blake put around my neck in Venice. I gaze at it as if hypnotized, but in fact I do not need the necklace. I recognize the man. Brian, the one who felled Rupert.

'Can I take my hand off now?'

I nod.

'Take nothing. Just pick up your baby and keep him as quiet as you can,' he instructs.

Carefully I lift Sorab out of his crib and lay him across my chest. He makes a small sound, but does not wake up. We go down the stairs. The house is dark and silent. As we round the corner of the dining room, I see an inert shoe and quickly look away. I knew I had made a mistake from the moment I got into the car with those men. Now I know I am on the right path. Come what may. We get into the car and the car pulls away. I don't look back. I look down on Sorab's sleeping face and will him not to wake up, buy the noise of the helicopter blades wake him up. He screams his head off and does not stop until we touch down on a helipad in a totally different part of England.

Thirty-two

'Put your hand out for her to smell you,' says Brian.

The German shepherd looks at me warily. There is not an ounce of friendliness in her. This is the dog version of Mr. Barrington Senior.

I put my hand out.

'Guard,' Brian orders. The dog sniffs my hand and goes back into his sit position.

'Now, hold out your son's hand.'

I hesitate. Sorab's hands are so small and there is something about the dog that I don't quite trust. It has been trained to kill on command.

Brian turns to one of the other men and says, 'Give me your shoe.'

The man takes his shoe off and holds it out to Brian. He lets all four dogs sniff it. 'Guard,' he says, and throws the shoe into the air. It falls about thirty feet away. All four dogs run towards the shoe and form a circle around it, their backs to it.

'Go get your shoe back,' he tells the man.

The man begins walking towards his shoe. Five feet away from his shoe, the dogs growl viciously and bare their teeth. Their bodies are crouched, ready to pounce in attack. The man stops in his tracks.

'At ease,' Brian says, and in unison the dogs leave the shoe that they had been guarding so ferociously and trot back to him. He praises them then gives them treats.

'Let them smell the boy.'

I bend down and hold Sorab's hand out in front of their black faces. One by one they sniff his hand and go and sit by their master.

'Guard,' their master says. Immediately their ears stand to attention. Brian disappears and the dogs stay with Sorab and me as we catch the last of the day's sun. As soon as we go through the front door, the dogs stop following us and begin patrolling the grounds.

It has been two days that we are living in this house. It is surrounded by high walls, a massive manned gate, and teams of dogs that patrol the grounds incessantly. There are CCTV cameras every few yards and security staff watching their screens twenty-four hours a day.

I wonder where Blake is and why he has not come for me, but I feel no fear. I know Sorab and I are safe here. I think about Billie. There is no way to contact her either. There is no Internet or a phone line. That evening I dine alone and go to bed early. I feel lonely but I am not bored. I know that somewhere out there Blake is executing the plans that I have seen so many times in his eyes.

It is 2:00 am when I feel the mattress depress next to me.

'Blake?'

'Who else did you expect?'

Thirty-three

I lunge into his arms with a yelp of pure joy and rain kisses on him; his lips, his cheeks, his eyelids, his hands. 'I'm sorry, I'm so sorry I ran away. I thought I was doing the right thing.'

'It's all right. I knew you would. Once you sold yourself for your mother. I knew you would do the same for me.'

I cannot hold back the tears. He did understand. I had no choice. I had to break my promise to him.

'I love you, Lana Bloom, I love you more than life itself.'

'Oh, darling. I've waited so long to hear you say that.'

'I've loved you for a very long time. I thought you'd know. My every action screamed it. Even when I thought you left, I couldn't forget you. We have this unbreakable connection. No matter what you do, I still long for you. I always have and I always will. Could you 'not tell?'

'Maybe, but I couldn't be sure. Why couldn't you tell me?'

'Because I wanted my father to think the relationship was temporary. It gave me time to lay down my plans.'

'If you had told me I wouldn't have told anyone, anyway.'

'And take the risk that you would blurt it out accidentally in a conversation with Billie or Jack? No, the stakes were too high. It involved you.'

'Will you tell me everything now?'

For a moment he hesitates.

'Please.'

He nods and switches on the bedside lamp, and suddenly I see how worn he looks. There is also a look in his eyes that I wish wasn't there. It is the look of a man who has had to tell the vet to end his beloved dog's suffering. I lay my palm on his cheek. 'Are you OK?'

'Yes. I was always safe. You were the one in danger.'

'As you can see, I am just fine.'

He takes a deep breath, his chest collapsing. 'Oh, God, the thought that you might not have been.'

'How did you know where to send Brian?'

'Our apartment was bugged, not only by my father, but by me too. I knew he had been around and what he had told you.'

'So you knew when we were at The Ritz that I was leaving you the next day.'

He nods.

'Why didn't you try to stop me?'

'The only thing I had on my side was the element of surprise.'

'Where is your father now?'

His eyes harden. 'As of fifteen minutes ago, the victim of a plane crash.'

'You killed him,' I gasp, utterly horrified.

'Yes,' he admits flatly.

'Why?' My voice is no more than a whisper.

'Because he wanted to terminate the thing I love most in the world. And what my father wants, my father gets.'

'You killed your father for me?' My voice is incredulous, disbelieving. The words I waited so long to hear, tainted.

'The real test of love is not being willing to kill for someone, but being able to give up your own life for them. I think I proved my love for you more than a year ago.'

'Oh no, what have you done?' I close my eyes in horror. 'He wasn't going to kill me. He just wanted me out of your life. He was only going to set me up with a new identity.'

'My little innocent. How little you know us. It is cheaper and far less troublesome to kill someone of little value than to give them a new identity and support them for life.'

I shake my head. I am in a state of shock. Blake killed his own father. I can't take it in. Everything is screwed up. 'Will you have to go to prison?'

He smiles sadly. 'How many billionaires do you know languishing in prison cells?'

'So you killed him,' I say again. As if repeating it will somehow make it go away.

'And would again.'

'Why did he hate me so much?'

'He didn't hate you, Lana. You were simply in his way. He wanted Sorab.'

Thirty-four

I wear this crown of thorns
Upon my liar's chair
Full of broken thoughts
I cannot repair.
—Hurt, Johnny Cash's Version
http://www.youtube.com/watch?
v=SmVAWKfJ4Go

'Sorab?' I gasp, utterly, utterly confused.

'You were looking for Cronus. Did you find him?' he asks sadly.

'Your father told me I should be looking for El.'

'And did you?'

I shake my head. I can't remember the details. All my

thoughts are scattered and ruffled. 'Only briefly. There was not enough time. It used to be the name of the highest god before it became a generic name for God.'

'Mmnnn.' But he is not really listening. He turns away from me, and rests his forehead on the heel of his palm. 'Remember when my father told you, his father was a banker, he is a banker, and his son will be a banker. Well, here is something he didn't tell you. My father has a dead brother, I have a dead brother and Sorab's brother would have had a dead brother too.'

I feel the blood drain away from my face. I grasp his arm and turn him to face me. 'What are you telling me?'

His eyes. His eyes. I become terrified. Not of him, but for him.

'What did your Wikipedia tell you was the demand of the highest god?'

My fingers are icy. 'Sacrifice of the first-born.' My eyes narrow. 'Are you trying to tell me that your family are Satanists?'

'No, that is for the rough and the crude. A show. We are the sons of El.'

I shrink from him, feeling like one of those boys who dive for pearls, get entangled in seaweed, and run out of breath. 'Wait, just wait for one moment. I can't take any of this in. I'm sorry I just can't. It's making me feel sick.' And it is too. I feel my stomach heave even though there is nothing in it.

'We count on people to be incredulous, to turn away because it is too terrible to contemplate. It is our protection. Do you still want the truth, Lana? Do you want to know what a monster I am, or shall we go back to what we were? We can pretend I am your knight in shining armor. That you made the right choice when you accepted my offer over Rupert's. Your choice.'

I take a deep breath. The shock made me react in that way. I want the truth. The whole truth. No more lies. No more pretenses. If I kick hard enough I will reach the surface and the light.

'I want the truth, whatever it may be,' I tell him.

'People think that they are no different from us, that we are all playing for the same stakes. That by a process of aspiration and hard work, perhaps a lucky break they can become one of us. Nothing could be further from the truth.

'We are not merely different we are a different species entirely. We are willing to go further than anybody else. Our naked ambition is a cold vise-like clamp around our hearts that causes us to align ourselves to a horrific blackness. And the blackness craves power over others and maintains itself by sucking the innocent energies of others.'

My heart is thudding so hard in my chest I can hear its roar in my ears.

'A child goes missing every three minutes in the United Kingdom alone, and around the world millions disappear every year. They are never seen, heard of or found. What do you think happens to them?'

I am too stunned to reply.

'On some days of the year, but especially eight dates, tens of thousands of children are sacrificed, not just by the sons of El, obviously, but by the Satanist and other cults around the world. On the night of the autumn equinox, September 21, three days from today, Sorab would have been ritually murdered. Like my brother, his uncle, and his uncle before him.'

My hands are clasped like a prayer in front of my mouth.

'I had to stop it,' he says, his face gray.

'Why couldn't we have just run away? Why have his blood on our hands?'

'There is no place on earth where Sorab, or you, for that matter, would have been safe. Only with me at the helm of the agenda, can the forces be held back.'

'But I don't want you at the helm of such a sick and twisted religion,' I cry.

'There is no other way. It is not a club. We are chosen to rule. I was born into it and must die in it.' I shudder visibly. 'Please,' he continues, 'don't grieve for me. I am reconciled to the knowledge that it shall be for me...a hell for all eternity. It is only important now that Sorab and any other children I father are not initiated. They will be free as my brother Quinn is.'

My skull aches. 'Is Marcus involved in...your father's death?'

'No. I acted alone. To protect what is mine.'

A desperate sob escapes me. 'Why can't we run away and let Marcus take over? He's older than you.'

'Marcus is not strong. My father always knew that. It was always going to me. At the helm of this empire of dirt.'

'Why can't you expose them? Tell the whole world the truth.'

'Who would I tell, Lana? Over the years hundreds of children who have escaped have told the same story, with the same details of underground chambers, hooded figures, orgies, and sacrificial murders, and they have all been dismissed as unreliable fantasists. Not a single figure of real prominence has ever been brought to justice.'

'But you are Barrington. You are powerful. You have inside information. You know people. You are not an unreliable witness.'

'The other families would immediately close ranks. What my father claimed he would do to me will be done. I will be destroyed and you and Sorab will disappear without a trace.'

I am frightened to ask my next question, my throat feels raw. I swallow. 'Do you also participate in these... rituals?'

'No, the rituals are not for us. We float above them. They are for the compromised and those who enjoy such perversions. I do not.'

'Can you not stop the agenda from the inside out?'

'Can *you* stop Monday from rolling into Tuesday? No one can stop the agenda, Lana. It will come to pass no matter what I do.'

Thirty-five

I fell into a burning ring of fire
I went down, down, down as the flames went higher
And it burns, burns, burns,
The ring of fire, the ring of fire.
—*The Ring of Fire*, Johnny Cash

That night we do not make love.

We huddle together like the shell-shocked survivors in the embers of a horrific battlefield. All around us are the dead and the terrible cries and wails of the dying. His hands cling to mine.

His voice is a whisper in my hair. 'I know I should push you away, but I can't. Until you came I lived a joyless life. It will be up to you to leave me.'

Finally, I understand why the choice to stay will be mine.

It is only in the early morning hours that his hands stop clinging, relax, and fall away in exhausted sleep, but sleep never comes for me. I lie on my side, his warm body curled around me and I think of Victoria's mother. That shrill look in her eyes that had so frightened me. She was right. It was already too late for me by the time she came to see me.

When the first light filters through the gap in the curtains I watch him sleep, his face relaxed and vulnerable, and I shiver not with desire, but with the memory of my desire for this man, for this body. It seems another lifetime ago. I think of what he has done for Sorab and I, and I am filled with sorrow at the thought of the secrets and sins that he carries in his soul. I understand that he is as trapped as I was when I slipped into a sluttish orange dress and went to sell my body to the highest bidder.

Billie, Jack, and probably even you...you thought it was too much to sacrifice for such a small percentage of success, didn't you? But I didn't. I would have done anything for my mother. Would I kill for her? If someone climbed into her bedroom and threatened her survival, yes, in a heart beat. Blake and I are worlds apart and yet we are cut from the same cloth.

I get dressed quietly and put my son into his carrycot. He smiles at me. I look into his clear blue eyes and feel like sobbing. How lucky he is. He is pure. He has done nothing wrong, yet.

I go downstairs.

Brian is sitting at the kitchen table watching TV. It is running the news of Blake's father's plane crash. When he sees me at the doorway, he switches off the telly and stands up. In his eyes something has changed. A new respect. It is in recognition of my association with the new head of the Barrington empire.

'Good morning, Ma'am.'

Ma'am? Even that's new. 'Good morning, Brian. Is there a church nearby?'

'Sure, but it won't be open yet. Bit early.'

'Can we try it, anyway?'

'Of course. Would you like to go now?'

'Yes.'

'I'll let Steve know.'

Outside Tom is carefully polishing the Bentley.

'Good morning, Miss. Bloom,' he calls.

I wave.

Brian drives me to the church, and as luck would have it, a man is locking the great doors. I run up to him, carrycot in hand.

'Oh please, please. Can I go in and say a quick prayer?'

He looks at me, glances at the child. Behind his gold-rimmed glasses his eyes are kind, innocent, unaware that I have been touched by sin. Would he believe me if I told about the secret world of the children of El? What they do for power and domination? Even to me, in the cold light of day, it all seems like a fantastical nightmare or a particularly bad film script.

He smiles kindly, and opens the door.

'Thank you. Thank you very much.'

'I'll be outside. Go with God, my child.'

Inside it is very quiet. First, I consecrate myself with holy water, then I walk down the old church. Light is filtering in through the stained glass, a magnificent aspect in the still gloom of grey stone. It streams onto a massive icon of the dying Christ as he hangs sorrowing above the altar. Above the smell of flowers and ferns.

I stand in silent awe in the middle of the house of God. A lost sheep returning to its fold. Alone, I go to the side of the hall where there is a statue of Mary carrying baby Jesus in her arms. I open a wooden box and take out four candles. They cost a pound each, but I have no money with me. I will come back tomorrow and put the four pounds into their donation box. I light the candles and put them into their metal holders. One for Jack, one for Sorab and one for Blake and one for all the little children.

The flames cast their warm light into the shadows.

I remember my grandmother saying, Gods are not beings like people. It is only humans who have given them arms and legs and faces. They are metaphors for all the things human consciousness can aspire to. If there is a darkness called El, then there must be another metaphor to describe the consciousness of light and goodness. I will pray to that god, in every temple, mosque, synagogue and church that I find.

I fall to my knees, cross myself and pray.

'Dear God, take care of Jack while he is in war-torn Africa and bring him back to this kind land as soon as possible.'

I stand and put the carrycot with Sorab in it in front of the altar and return my knees to the cold stone floor.

'I give you my son to keep safe for always and…in return, I promise to do for the little children all that is in my power…until my last breath. I am not a cog in the machine. I am not a bloodline. I can make a difference. Nothing is set in stone. Not even the agenda.'

Then I bow my head and pray for Blake's tormented soul. With the unyielding, cold stone against my knees, I tell God, 'Dear God, this is my sincere and most fervent prayer, if Blake must burn in hell for eternity, then I must burn with him. For we are two souls that must never again be parted.'

"Some of the biggest men in the United States, in the field of commerce and manufacture, are afraid of somebody, are afraid of something. They know that there is a power somewhere so organized, so subtle, so watchful, so interlocked, so complete, so pervasive, that they had better not speak above their breath when they speak in condemnation of it."

Thomas Woodrow Wilson
28th President of the United States (1913 to 1921)

About the Author

Thank you to all you awesome readers who left feedback and reviews for The Billionaire Banker. Reviews are incredibly precious to new authors as they help other readers find the book.

As a gesture of gratitude the first hundred Amazon reviewers for *42 Days* will get the next book (Yay! out in May) as a gift from me, with love. Just leave an honest review on Amazon, then write to me at

Georgialecarre@gmail.com   or

Facebook.com/georgialecarre

to tell me you have done so and Voilà...

See you at the back of the next book. But until then, say hello to a beautiful stranger, he could ignore you or marry you...

Georgia   xx

CPSIA information can be obtained
at www.ICGtesting.com
Printed in the USA
LVHW04s1432020718
582500LV00001B/400/P